2ᵒᵒ

AFTER THE WORLD ENDED

"We date the beginning of the Modern Era from the Great War of the North...the suffering that then befell the earth was immense. A first-century Swede must have spoken for most of the north when he wrote of the war: 'The gods and giants battled over all the world and made a wasteland which the heroes of a thousand years will not cure; the Midgard serpent shook the earth in his coils and spat venom on those who chanced to survive; the sun herself was swallowed up in the maw of the wolf and ceased to shine on mankind, summer though it was.'"

WINTER'S DAUGHTER

"Terrific, a special book, a powerful fusion of Norse saga and science fiction...Signe is a hero for her times!"
Michael Swanwick, author of *In the Drift*

"Altogether admirable...totally unlike any other postapocalyptic SF novel I can think of."
Scott Baker, author of *Dhampire*

WINTER'S DAUGHTER

The Saying of
Signe Ragnhilds-datter.

CHARLES WHITMORE

 AVON
PUBLISHERS OF BARD, CAMELOT, DISCUS AND FLARE BOOKS

AVON BOOKS
A division of
The Hearst Corporation
1790 Broadway
New York, New York 10019

Copyright © 1984 by Charles Whitmore
Published by arrangement with Pocket Books
Library of Congress Catalog Card Number: 83-18111
ISBN: 0-380-70117-0

The Timescape Books/Simon & Schuster edition contains the following Library of Congress Cataloging in Publication Data:

Whitmore, Charles.
  Winter's daughter.

  I. Title.
PS3573.H525W5   1984   813'.54   83-18111

First Avon Printing: December 1986

AVON TRADEMARK REG. U.S. PAT. OFF. AND IN OTHER COUNTRIES, MARCA REGISTRADA, HECHO IN U.S.A.

Printed in the U.S.A.

K-R 10 9 8 7 6 5 4 3 2 1

Contents

Introduction

We date the beginning of the Modern Era from the Great War of the North, called Ragnarok—the Twilight of the Gods—in Scandinavia, or the Trial by Fire (Armageddon) in North America. The suffering that then befell the earth was immense, especially so for the proud nations of the north. Disease and famine followed the war, and in the end left nine of every ten northerners dead—as well as a devastation so vast that its marks can still be seen. A first-century Swede must have spoken for most of the north when he wrote of the war: "The gods and giants battled over all the world and made a wasteland which the heroes of a thousand years will not cure; the Midgard serpent shook the earth in his coils and spat venom on those who chanced to survive; the sun herself was swallowed up in the maw of the wolf, and ceased to shine on mankind, summer though it was." In the words of a North American, "Happy the corpse who never saw what I have seen."

The longer historical consequences of the war have been no less important. Economic vitality and military strength have shifted irrevocably southward; the world's destiny is shaped in São Paulo and Lagos, Nairobi and Delhi, no longer in Washington, Paris, and Moscow. The once-mighty world of the white man entered an eclipse from which it shows few signs of emerging.

Students of literature have long been attracted to prewar European cultures. Until recently, however, few thought it worthwhile to study the works of the postwar period. Even now, that time lives in the public imagination as one of virtually unrelieved misery and barbarity; even scholarly criticism all too often does no more than elaborate J. P. F. Munyuku's dictum: "Postwar white art has all the appeal of a dead incinerator."

However true Munyuku's judgment may be for the first decades of the Modern Era (a time certainly marked by near-universal chaos and frequent religious persecution), it is patently wrong when applied to the second century, the so-called False Dawn period. Throughout most of that century, literature flourished in the northern lands of Scandinavia and Wisconsin; painting, music, and sculpture in lands further to the south. The Dawn was as fragile as it was fertile, lasting barely more than a century before succumbing to the Plague Wars early in the third century. But the period's accomplishments were anything but fleeting.

The literature of the False Dawn has been neglected longer than its other artistic forms, largely because so few scholars have been able to read the various Scandinavian tongues (or the Middle American dialect of English, for that matter). In recent years the works of the Dawn have become somewhat more widely read through the erudite, if occasionally arcane, translations of Martin D. B. Ntukamazina. Some of the writing has by now attracted sufficient critical and popular acclaim to justify a new translation for the more general African audience.

The Saying of Signe Ragnhilds-datter

The Saying of Signe Ragnhilds-datter (or Winter's Daughter) is easily the most panoramic of all False Dawn works. The story begins with the separate arrivals of Signe's parents, Ragnhild (a Norwegian) and Michael (an American), in Africa shortly before the war. It follows the fortunes of this couple and their children during the aftermath of the war in Africa and through their wanderings later in America and Norway.

The breadth of interest displayed in Winter's Daughter is a salutary reminder that even in the poverty of postwar Scandinavia, people saw a world much wider than their own homelands. Winter's Daughter also provides a glimpse of our own East African history as seen through foreign eyes—a fact that makes it in some ways the most accessible of the False Dawn works.

Winter's Daughter was probably composed in the decade between 105 and 115 M. E. (Modern Era), placing it in the earliest period of the False Dawn. Two archaic qualities of the text can easily be seen: the style is still unusually spare, and there are no references to other postwar works, with the single exception of the *Memoirs of Stephen the Nearly Lucky*, a predawn American source.

The author of Winter's Daughter is unknown (anonymity was customary during the Scandinavian Dawn), but clearly had access to a large store of family history. This fact has led most scholars to the perhaps pedestrian conclusion that the writer must have been a descendant of the heroine. The most likely candidates are Ragnhild Michaels-datter and Finn Eiriks-son. Finn is known to have traveled widely as a youth, primarily on trading expeditions, but it is unlikely that he ever got so far as Wisconsin. On the whole, the attribution to Ragnhild seems the more likely; she also traveled widely and had the reputation of being "that most clever of women." In any case, few scholars still credit the once-popular theory that the work must have had two authors.

Whoever wrote Winter's Daughter lived in the west of Norway, in the upper reaches of Hardanger fjord, not far from the family's old farm at Eidfjord. He or she wrote for a local audience and often took for granted details of law and geography, not only about Norway, but also (oddly) about North America. The narrative is seldom difficult to follow, but I have taken the liberty of including maps and introductions at the beginning of each major section.

Acknowledgments

This work could not have been undertaken without the encouragement and complicity of the Dead Languages Institute of Mombasa, Kenya. Many of the translations offered here have benefited from the help of my colleagues there. I invite their shared responsibility for any errors that remain.

Thanks are also due to my archive operator, P. L. Kuuya, whose help has been invaluable and irreplicable.

G. K. ULAYA
Mombasa, Kenya
23 March 449 M. E.

❄ Part One
Africa

Michael Flanagan

There was a man called Michael Flanagan, an American from Wisconsin who found himself in Africa for the Fenris sun. He was a brown-haired man and hearty, thirty winters old and with crinkled eyes. Michael spent most the years before the war at home in America and married a woman called Mathilda. In time she came to nag at him, until, in the end, he left her. Mathilda's father took the matter badly and hired some men to kill Michael if they could find him.

Michael thought it best after that to move to Tanzania. There he lived in Dar es Salaam from the second year before the war; and there, stayed by fate, he finished his life in after days.

It is said that in those days Michael had eyes for married women and for no others. He had poor luck on most his quests, however, even when he was most in earnest. People laughed at him for this and called him the cat who knew many windows, but only from the outside. The American was also fond of the things he owned, particularly of a great oaken desk, dark with age, and of a carpet he had brought all the way from Turkey. Michael let no one walk on his carpet, and many laughed at him for this also.

Indeed, it is said that most Africans thought Michael something of a fool. However that is, Michael found friends in Dar es Salaam, the closest a Tanzanian called Zachias Mwakalinga. Zachias was a priest of Christ and, through the church, a man of

11

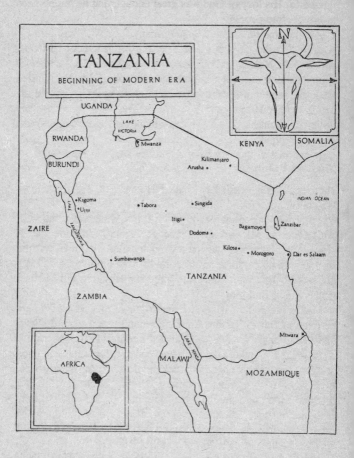

TANZANIA
BEGINNING OF MODERN ERA

the world. His love of God was great enough that he felt no need to bow before people.

Zachias had the habit of asking many friends to join him for feasts where he gave them beer he brewed himself. This beer was widely hailed for both strength and taste, but Zachias let people drink it only after ten minutes or more of thanksgiving to God. He sometimes went so far as to give thanks for the beasts of the field, one by one.

Once, Michael asked his friend why he said such long prayers. Zachias replied, "When people think much on the works of God, they get thirsty; then the prayer ends by blessing the beer."

Ragnhild Arnes-datter

A Norsewoman from Eidfjord, called Ragnhild Arnes-datter, also saw Ragnarok from Africa. She was a doctor who had fared widely in the years before Thor's bane, to Bergen and Iceland, at last to a place called Bagamoyo in Tanzania. This town lay on the coast, two hours north from Michael's house in Dar es Salaam.

Ragnhild was a tall woman and redding blond. She seldom let things go for long in a way she didn't like, though she got on well with people as a rule. Even so, there was but a single person she trusted in Bagamoyo.

This was Matthew Basumingera, a Tanzanian whose family had come from west of the Great Lake of Africa. Matthew was a tall man and one who could run forever. He seemed odd to his neighbors because he chose to live the life of the poor: he ate only rice, fish, and fruit, even on feast days. But many people liked his voice, which sounded a sort of music.

Matthew spent his spare hours working with some villagers nearby in a common yard. He got them to share the crop according to who had worked for it rather than to reputation; he also gave the village its first football. But the government came annoyed with Matthew's work off and then, especially one time when the village refused to plant what the government asked, but thought instead to buy their own seed with the money they had from working the field with Matthew.

Matthew and Ragnhild were good friends, however, from the time Ragnhild helped cure his malaria. Matthew was as well cousin to Michael's friend Zachias, the priest of Christ.

There lived as well in Bagamoyo a man called Georg Mueller. He came from Switzerland, a short man, well-favored for looks, dark-haired, and with a strong nose. He knew everything about the machines around him and thought he knew as much of the people. Georg was quick to act, and sometimes cruel. Other people usually felt less love than fear for him.

Georg took it on himself to love Ragnhild Arnes-datter. He found the way to her house often, and brought many things to give her. But Ragnhild would say no more than was polite.

Once Georg said, "Tell me why it is that you've never married."

"I've not met the man I'd like to live a long time with," replied Ragnhild, "and I can think that won't soon change, either."

"And I can hope that it already has."

"Then your hopes are different from mine."

Another time, when Georg was often seen at Ragnhild's house, Matthew asked his Norse friend, "Why keep your door open to the man when he's such a nuisance?"

Ragnhild answered, "It's better for him to be a fool than for me to be rude."

Two Visits to Michael

Ragnhild's friend Matthew Basumingera sometimes went to Dar es Salaam to share in Zachias's feast days. It happened one time that Ragnhild went with him. This was at the last Yule before the dark days.

Michael Flanagan was among those at the feast. He saw Ragnhild when first she came in and said to Zachias, "I wonder if you'll tell me who this woman is? She seems more than a bit handsome to me."

The priest replied, "You don't often say that of a single woman." But he introduced the two all the same.

Michael and Ragnhild spoke together for some time, but there was little to show how she thought of him. Ragnhild mentioned that she meant to stay on in Dar es Salaam for some days after Yule. Michael said, "It may be of no use to you, but I have the room for you to stay in my house if you like."

"I don't make a habit of ignoring such kindness," said Ragnhild, "but you'll deserve whatever you get from it."

Matthew went home two days later. Ragnhild had no wish to trouble Zachias further; she went to Michael's house instead and stayed there three days longer. Ragnhild and Michael were friendly enough during that time. But when Ragnhild made ready to leave Dar es Salaam, she said, "Our talks together please me since you see what I mean better than most. But it's just as pleasing that you ask only to speak as friends; one man like Georg is enough for me."

Michael laughed and said, "I have my reputation to look after, in any case."

Ragnhild recame Bagamoyo and her own house late in the day. Georg came to greet her and said, "I thought you might like your letters."

"I've waited for them before, but thanks shall you have."

"I've also brought a bottle of wine we might share," said Georg.

"You know where the glasses are; as for me, I've had enough to drink the last few days. Beside, the journey was tiring."

Georg went to the kitchen and opened the bottle. But Ragnhild went into her own room and closed the door. Georg brought his wine back to an empty room. He drank one glass and knocked on Ragnhild's door. She said, "Please be at home, but I need my sleep."

"Yes," said Georg through the door. "It must be hard work to play with your boyfriend in Dar es Salaam. You can do as you like, of course, but it's a bad business when you tray an old friend like me."

Ragnhild opened the door and said, "You'll do better to talk of things you understand."

"And you've come pretty proud for a woman who's never been able to hold on to a man yet."

"One can't think the more highly of you, the more you talk."

"Then I'll leave you. But you shouldn't think I'll lie down as easily as one of your patients." Georg put his glass on the table and went out. It's said that he worked and drank more than usual after that.

Some time later, Georg himself went to Dar es Salaam, and on to Michael's house. He named himself and said, "I'm a friend of Ragnhild's; she said you might have a bed I could use for a day or two."

Michael replied, "I've heard your name; in any case, a friend of Ragnhild's is always welcome here."

"Yes," said Georg, "I thought things might be like that."

Georg stayed the night. In the morning he asked for an egg to eat. Michael said he had none to give: "You can't look for everything in this sort of hotel."

Georg said, "Perhaps not. But you have no call to come nasty with me."

The two men went out soon after. They saw no more of each other until the evening. Then they greeted each other well enough, and Georg brought a bottle of whiskey to share with his host; they drank several glasses together. Georg said, "I'd like to know one thing from you, and that's why it is you're stealing my woman."

Michael asked, "What are you thinking of?"

"You've no call not to know that I mean to marry Ragnhild when half the country's made of gossips. Yet still you want to make off with her yourself, as if she were some common whore."

"You're right that I like Ragnhild well. I doubt anyone will carry her off against her will, though."

The two continued drinking some time longer.

Georg said, "At the least you could tell me how her body is under the clothes." Michael gave no answer to that, but went on drinking his whiskey. Georg stood and walked about the room. After a time he stopped, spat at Michael's feet, and said, "The hell with you."

Michael said, "You had better go to a real hotel now; I can see that we're not getting on together."

"You're just the sort of pissant who'd shove a man out onto the street after drinking his liquor."

"Have it your way then." Michael went to his room and locked the door. But Georg slept where he lay.

In the morning, things were much as before. The two men met in the kitchen before breakfast. Georg said, "I'd like to take a shower if I may. It's enough that one of us stinks like half of Africa."

Michael gave him soap and a towel. Georg went to the shower; Michael borrowed three eggs from a neighbor and cooked them until the whites were hard. When Georg came back from cleaning himself Michael asked, "Are you still as interested in an egg as you were yesterday?"

Georg said that he was. "At least I can get something back from you."

"By all means," said Michael and pushed the eggs into Georg's face. Yellow and red drops soon ran down from the Swissman's nose.

Michael asked, "Would you like a napkin?"

"No, but I could use a knife."

"It's better if you leave instead and we speak no more of what's happened."

"I'm not about to do that when you've challenged me to a duel. At least you'll be more polite when we're done."

"You're a silly man," said Michael. "Still, I won't refuse to fight you after all these insults—so long as you choose weapons that won't kill us. I'd not like to lie in jail on your account."

"I'll tell you my choice this afternoon."

Georg left. He went home to Bagamoyo and asked a friend called Duane to act as second.

Michael went to Zachias the priest, told him what had happened, and said, "Now I need a friend to stand by me."

"I think you're the silly one," said Zachias. "You might as well be a tomcat for all the sense you show to fight when you haven't even a reason."

Michael replied, "What's done has to be lived with even so, and I need a second."

"So you come to a priest. You could exasperate anyone."

"It's not so bad, though, since the weapons have to be peaceful ones."

"Indeed," said Zachias. But he agreed to come, "though I'll have to think myself a seventeen-year-old again."

The Duel

Georg recame Michael's house late in the afternoon. He said, "I thought to use pellet guns to settle our dispute, but an American might know them too well. Beside, there's been little blood lost yet. I choose that we use violins."

Michael did not know what to answer for a moment, then said, "That may not be possible, since I've never tried to play a violin. Still, your mind must be mine in this."

"I've heard you're not much of a musician," said Georg. "But it's the better if you can't play. I'll try your crudeness and you my patience. You can use a toothbrush in place of the bow, if you like, and help your chances that way."

"That's most openhanded of you," said Michael.

They agreed to duel in this way: The fight would start at midnight the same evening. Each man would take turns playing for ten minutes. Either could break the other's music, but the first must still finish his time. When one or the other of them failed to take a turn, or to finish one, that man was lost.

At midnight all met: Georg; Michael; and the two in witness, Zachias and Duane. They gathered at Zachias's house in a room odd for that part of Africa. Its walls were wrapped in wood, yellow and brown, with many books on shelves backing them. Candles cut the darkness, but the moon was long set. Zachias said, "We are here as you two wished it, but it's my duty to ask if there isn't some way to make good your quarrel without wasting the night."

Georg said, "That is not easy when I've already wasted the day. But if you want terms, here they are. Michael must apologize to me for the disgrace of this morning; he must promise not to see Ragnhild again; and he must give me the carpet from his living room to show that he means well."

Duane said, "How do you answer these terms, Michael?"

Michael answered, "One thing's worse than the last. There's no choice but to fight, if he's going to insult me even now."

Duane said nothing to that, but brought two violin cases to the duelists. Michael opened the cases. On the right was a beautifully crafted violin that belonged to Georg. On the left was a plain instrument of Zachias's. Michael chose the second and said, "All instruments will sing the same for me."

Georg took his own violin. He had a bow with him, but Michael took a large toothbrush from Zachias.

Georg played first and easily for his ten minutes. Duane said he had seldom played better. Michael then took up the work. For a time he found it difficult to make any sound at all. What notes he chanced on trembled and clashed. But he finished his sixth of an hour; and such were the first blows.

The two men took turns playing for two hours without speaking or interrupting each other. Michael was then able to make some nasty sounds.

Then, quite suddenly, Michael screeched on his violin in the middle of a delicate part of Georg's playing. Georg said nothing and missed no note, but his lips went a little white. Michael played more happily after that, so Zachias thought he was taking the upper hand.

More time passed. Georg then broke into Michael's music and strung together some stray notes Michael had made by mistake. The tune played nicely; Georg came more cheerful than he had been. Michael almost missed his place, but seemed more grim than startled.

The duelists tired after they finished five hours of play. At last, one of Michael's noises upset Georg. The Swiss played a single very bad note and went on faster than he was used to. It seemed also that his hand trembled.

The sun began to color the sky soon after. It was about to break into open day when Michael began a turn. Georg stood, went to a cupboard, and took down four glasses. He filled them with brandy he had brought from Bagamoyo.

Michael's music took no note of movement, or of the sun's light when it fell on his face. At last he stopped; all sound stopped with him.

Georg said, "You have won; much good may it do you." He gave each man a glass. But Michael walked from the room instead.

Ragnhild's Answer

Georg went home later in the same day as the duel. There he called on Ragnhild. They sat at a table, and Georg said, "It's too bad your friend Michael can't be here. He fought a duel with me last night over you, but now he's too scared to come and talk about it." He told her how the fight had come about and what had happened when it was joined. He ended, "Now it seems you'll have to make do with me, even though I'm the loser."

"There you're wrong," said Ragnhild. "I need nothing from a slug, and certainly not from a foolish one. I'd rather talk with you no further, so it's best if you leave the house instead."

Georg began to laugh.

Ragnhild said, "Now."

The Swiss was unsure for a moment what to do. Then he rose and left the house. Ragnhild did not follow him to the door.

Ragnhild went to see her chief the next day. His name was Alexander Eleazer Rweyemamu. She said, "It may be that you've heard what Georg has been up to."

"It's not my job to rely on gossip."

Ragnhild told Alexander Eleazer some of what had happened. She then said, "Georg's always been a nuisance; now there's no trusting him at all. It's not safe if he and I live in the same place. I'd rather do my work someplace else."

"It's a pity when a rich doctor leaves the poor over some little quarrel. Still, it's not the first time."

"I've no wish to leave Tanzania over this," said Ragnhild. "The land needn't be any shorter of doctors than it already is. You've only to switch me for someone else."

Alexander Eleazer said, "I'll do what I can, but you give me scant reason to like Europeans any the better."

Matthew came to take his leave of Ragnhild. He said, "I'm glad that one never loses a friend, since I don't know when we may meet again."

"The Danes say, 'It's hard to make predictions, especially about the future,'" replied Ragnhild. "But we'll see each the other before many months pass."

"So one can hope," said Matthew. The conversation went on

to other things until Matthew said, "I doubt if Georg will lose much time coming to see me when he finds you're going. What will you have me tell him?"

"The truth, that I've gone, and it means nothing to him where. And also this, that I hope never to see him again."

At this time the great nations of the north readied their weapons and moved toward war. There was no fighting yet when Ragnhild left Bagamoyo, but many things did not work as usual; people looked only for the worst.

Ragnhild Visits Morogoro

Ragnhild came to Dar es Salaam. She could not find a way on to Norway, however. No one thought it wise to travel so far north as things stood.

Ragnhild made her way west instead, away from the sea, to a town called Morogoro. This was a place Georg seldom came. It is said that demons play in the skies around Morogoro and make the clouds purple and pink before storms. However that is, the land itself is peaceful enough.

Ragnhild stayed in a house in the hills that rise just south of the town. It was a solid house, and cool during the day, two miles by foot from the road.

Two other women stayed also in this house. One was a Tanzanian called Sara Mmari, a woman of middle height and strong-fingered. Sara killed insects for a living; she was come to Morogoro to show the people there how to rid themselves of pests. Most the time, she lived by the Deep Lake in a place called Kigoma. The other woman was named Evelyn Phillips. She was young, fair-haired, and English. Her parents had sent her to Morogoro because they thought it best that she see more of Africa than Dar es Salaam. She was not the most adventurous of people.

Ragnhild and Sara struck up a fast friendship. Evelyn stayed more to herself.

Georg Follows His Love

Georg heard that Ragnhild had left Bagamoyo. He went first to Alexander Eleazer and asked what had happened. But Alexander Eleazer said, "I can tell you I don't go around giving news to everyone who asks for it."

Georg went to Matthew then and asked if Ragnhild had told him anything of what she meant to do.

Matthew said that she had.

"What is it then?"

"That I can't tell you. But this I will, that you aren't likely to see her again and might as well turn your thoughts to other things."

Georg said, "I've gone through a lot for that woman; you won't talk me down from finding her now."

"That's up to you. But you won't get much good from it whether you find her or not."

Georg soon came to Dar es Salaam. He looked after his own business, then went to find what he could of Ragnhild. No one knew where she was. Some said she was mad and had set off to Europe by land; others thought she had gone to one part of Tanzania or another.

At last, Georg went to Michael Flanagan's house. Michael met him and said, "I didn't look to see you here."

Georg replied that he was on his way home and hoped only for some beer to make the way an easier one.

Michael said, "Yes, well. One can't refuse a small thing in hard times. After all, we may both be Africans soon."

"A poor fate that'd be," said Georg. But he had heard the news as well.

Michael gave Georg his beer and asked after one person and another. Finally, he asked if Ragnhild were well in Bagamoyo. It seemed he knew nothing of her journey.

"As to that," said Georg, "I've not heard her complain." He finished his beer, stood, and said, "I thank you for the drink, though it's small payment for the suffering you've brought me."

Michael asked Georg what he meant. Georg went a bit red in the face and said, "Don't play the fool with me. It's your doing that Ragnhild's disappeared."

Michael seemed confused. He started to ask another question. But by then Georg had taken him by the shirt and hit him full in the face. The blow was a hard one and broke the cheekbone. Michael fell to the floor. Georg said, "Paltry was your payment; so also is mine, but both will have to do."

Michael spent the next weeks in the sickhouse. His left eye was always sore in the sun after that. The only other thing told of Michael at this time is that he started to carve wooden masks to pass the time.

The Death of the North

Michael was still in bed when the skies of the north rained with bombs, and later when the clouds of dust first cloaked the earth. Some say that Fenris wolf then slipped his chains and ate the sun. Odin, weak from his thousand-year sleep at the foot of Christ's cross, also woke and killed the wolf, but got mortal wounds doing so. After that, all evil broke its bonds and killed both the old gods and most the people of the north. Only high valor and luck led the doomed gods to fight on against their foes. But this they did until there were too few evils left to stop the birth of a new heaven and a new earth and the laughing children of the gods themselves.

However one listens to the old tales, all know that the sun shone with ill light for three full days, and that the moon was a mere blue shape of herself. Many were already dead, but those who lived on forgot themselves even more than at first, so that brothers killed each the other for scraps of meat. Worse still came when the earth itself turned on people and let little grow of what was always there before. The air also carried illness; many were those who breathed at the wrong time and sickened away to death, even those who were most healthy and clever, they as well. People found that their bodies betrayed them. Many women gave birth to dead children, and others found monsters grown in their wombs, planted by devils unseen. Some lived through the first bad times to find themselves envying the dead; some were blind, but others heard more than sounded. Some found lumps growing on them and soon were caught in cancer's claw. Even before most the lumps showed themselves, bulges of new sickness broke over the land every few years. In the worst of these, people fevered and turned gray; in three days they could no longer walk; in five they were dead.

The Christians say that God sent a judgment to the world for its bad ways in the old times. They say that all must be grateful that He spared the time to deal with a small matter before it came so bad that all had to die. They also call the pagan stories foolish and say that all people would do better to look to their own souls than to repeat frivolous tales.

Whoever has the right of these stories, all people know that the south sapped strength from the war, and that people there were free from the worst. Ragnhild, Sara Mmari, and Evelyn knew nothing in their mountain retreat till the sky went dark. Then Evelyn grew fearful and could not sleep. She decided to make her way back to her parents in Dar es Salaam, by foot if need be.

Ragnhild heard of this and told Evelyn that it was not safe to walk under the sky as it was now. And Sara Mmari said, "There are also those on the road and in the towns who've always hated white faces. They won't hold themselves back any more."

In the end, Evelyn gave in. She still thought it bad form to leave off crying, however, and stayed in her room most the time. But Ragnhild and Sara talked together and played darts through the evenings. Ragnhild soon came good enough at this to win when she wanted to.

The three women stayed together through the time of the long rains. The rains were unusually heavy that year.

Early in June, Sara Mmari made ready to leave. Ragnhild now asked her what a European woman might best do next.

"Stay with this Evelyn for now," replied Sara, "and go back to your people in Dar es Salaam. They're as close to family as you come now."

"I've not had much in common with them before," said Ragnhild.

"Maybe not. But you'll need more than a few African friends before you find a home here."

"My grandchildren may have a home," said Ragnhild. "As for me, I look for other things."

Sara waited a moment and then said, "Go as you must. But my house will be yours, if someday you come on worse times than these."

Ragnhild and Sara exchanged presents and parted on the best of terms.

Soon after, Ragnhild and Evelyn also left Morogoro and traveled together to Dar es Salaam. Evelyn asked Ragnhild to stay with her and her parents for a time. She thought her parents might have come strangers. Ragnhild agreed to stop with the family until she could tell more of what the future held.

After some weeks, Matthew Basumingera came to Dar es Salaam from Bagamoyo. Evelyn's father was a man named Trevor. He heard of Matthew's visit and that Ragnhild was an old friend of his. He said to Ragnhild, "The police don't like this Matthew of yours. It's not the safest thing for you to be seen talking with him."

"Probably not," said Ragnhild. "But it's trouble worth the having, if being his friend brings it."

Ragnhild met Matthew at the beach where he liked to buy fish. They spoke of many things. At last, Ragnhild asked, "What news is there from Alexander Eleazer?"

"He says things move slowly when so many have to decide about something."

"He's never been one to bend rules far."

"No. And in this case, he's not sent the letter to have you moved. He says it's not his job to waste the effort when you might be so fickle as to come back."

"That's not very likely," said Ragnhild, "though it's better to work than not."

"I'd stay away, if I were you. Georg is no better than you can remember, and Alexander Eleazer has said as much bad as good of you."

"Still, I haven't any good place to go otherwise. I can't stay with Trevor any longer, and I can't have a house of my own till I find work."

Matthew asked, "What of that man Michael you once spoke well of? He might help with one thing or another."

Ragnhild thought a moment and said, "I'll go to see him as you say, but it's hard to know if we'll still be friends. He's not the one I'd choose to bother, if I had the choice."

Matthew and Ragnhild parted with the promise to stand each by the other, as far as was possible.

Ragnhild came to Michael's house later that same afternoon. The American met her at the door and said, "You're as welcome a guest as any I could hope for, though I hardly looked to see you again." He gave her a chair in the living room and a cup of tea. Then he said, "Tell me how you come here now."

Ragnhild told Michael some of her story and said, "I remember that you once said I might stay here in peace; I wonder if that's still true, now that the world's so changed?"

"You're as welcome now as then," said Michael, "and for so long as you like."

"I'll take your offer up, in that case. I must tell you first, though, that I have no use for your fight with Georg. No one helps me by doing such things, and I won't be slow to leave if you try."

"That's up to you," replied Michael. "But I fight only for my own sake, and not very well at that. As for you, I imagine you can take care of your own problems."

"Better than most," said Ragnhild Arnes-datter. She moved to Michael's house on the day following; she and Michael gave each other a wide berth for the following months. But mealtimes were friendly enough.

Europeans Take Their Leave

Life was safer for Europeans in Africa by the beginning of the following year. Also by then, the governments of African lands had to decide how they should be treated. The Europeans were wealthy and well trained from having been many years to school. They were also used to high living, and this fact often affronted Africans.

The leaders of Tanzania met. In the end, they decided that all the whites who wished could stay in the country; but they must give up their high wages, pay a special tax, and do whatever work the government asked of them for seven years. Those who would rather leave the country might do that as well; but they could take but a few things with them.

The head of Tanzania gave this speech: "We Tanzanians believe that all people have dignity, wherever they come from, and whatever gods they pray to. Our country stands ever ready to shelter those in need, even if their lands were not always so open with us. Our hearts fly most to those who gave much in their own eyes to come here and help us build the nation.

"But we are not stupid people. Many of these Europeans came not to help us but to enrich themselves. They are not the first to do so, but follow in many ugly footsteps.

"We welcome those who will live among us as equals and take a full share in our work. The others, the ones who want to prey on our pity as once they plundered our weakness, those we send away without mercy, and their thoughts of gain at the expense of others with them."

Many Europeans had scant liking for these words, or for the laws behind them. Some went to South Africa, and Georg Mueller among them, because that place was rich and ruled by whites still. Others thought South Africa scarcely civilized and went north to Kenya; or in case that they spoke better French than English, they crossed the Deepest Lake to Zaire with its great river.

Ragnhild went to Michael while all the Europeans weighed what to do. She said, "You should tell me plainly how all this strikes you. I'll need to find a new house, if you mean to leave."

"There's no need for that," answered Michael, "unless you're tired of my company."

"You might get better help for your eye in some other place."

"That's possible. Still, I'm content to take no more than is mine by right. I like this place, and my friends are here."

Ragnhild laughed at this and said, "I sometimes think we understand each other better than we like to say."

By this time Ragnhild had work and was well thought of in her job. Michael was as healthy as he was like to come. It is said of him that he spoke less than in the old days, but with greater weight.

Ragnhild and Michael

Ragnhild and Michael married in the year following. They had two children together, a daughter called Signe and a son, Edvard.

Signe was the older by three years. Both were promising children, quick to learn and well-favored to the eye. Otherwise they had little in common; Edvard took the light look of his mother, but Signe had darker hair.

Signe was the favorite of Matthew Basumingera. He often came to Dar es Salaam and took her swimming in the ocean. Sometimes he also went to sea with the fishermen and brought his niece with him. But Zachias Mwakalinga the priest liked Edvard the better because he was the younger.

No more is told of these children until the year when Signe was nine years old. One day shortly before Fool's Day, it happened that Edvard and a friend of his called Mwita played in the grass beside the house.

A lizard came from the next yard, a large reptile the size of a cat. Mwita and Edvard both saw it at once; they began to scream. Signe and several other children came to them, but the lizard kept coming closer. At last Signe took a stick and chased the lizard away. It fled into the street and under a car. The creature died at once.

As it happened, this lizard belonged to a man called Abdul. Abdul liked his lizard because it was rare. He came directly to Michael's house and asked to be repaid. He said, "I'll need money to find a new one, but money alone won't make good the loss."

Michael replied, "I'm happy to give you the money you ask, since we've always been friends. You're more than welcome to my apology as well."

"I think it was someone else who hurt me," said Abdul. "I'd rather hear it from her."

Ragnhild brought Signe into the room. Abdul asked the girl to beg forgiveness for driving the lizard into the street. But Signe would say nothing.

Ragnhild said to Signe, "It's good to let neighbors know that you take their feelings to heart."

Signe answered her mother, "I think you might take my feelings to heart when I look after Edvard, who's still so young."

To Abdul she said, "I killed your friend. But I'll not say I'm sorry of it."

Abdul again asked her to apologize; Signe said, "I've done what I've done. You won't get me to give it up."

Abdul went home without hearing the word he had come for.

Piero and Mohammed

There was at this time in Dar es Salaam a man called Piero, a thin fellow, half-Italian and half-Danish, born to a look of sadness. He could find no place of his own in the world before the war; so he fared to Tanzania. He soon came a valued man because he did many services no one else would try.

Soon after the bombs burst over the north, however, Piero's wife Anna killed herself. Piero soon took to gambling, and some years later lost his job; the Tanzanians saw no reason to pay him for work he seldom did. They let him stay on in the country, however, because of the good he had done before. Piero lived in an old house with two servants. The government gave him a pension; otherwise he made a living however he could.

Piero came to Michael's house soon after Yule one year. This was the time when Signe was fourteen and Edvard eleven. Edvard did all the things he should and let no one know his thoughts, but Michael had more fondness for his firstborn.

Piero asked for money. Michael replied, "I'm not about to pay for a man who does as little good as you, though I can think well of your nerve."

Piero replied, "It's likely you don't know how bad a man I've come. You can be sure to see me more, though, if you won't give any better answer now."

Michael refused to say more; there the matter rested for the time being.

. . .

There was also a youth named Mohammed, an Arab and the son of a tailor. He was a clever lad, among the best at school, and always ready to do odd bits of work for money. He had pride in his smooth face and seemed a pleasant enough sort. It was said of him, however, that he carried no principle far.

Some time after Piero went to Michael for money, he also thought to have his house painted. It had gone many years without. He asked Mohammed to take the work if he liked it, and promised to pay the work's worth and more.

Mohammed agreed and started to work at once. He finished the job with no time wasted. But Piero had no money for him when the time came to settle accounts. Said Piero, "It seems to me you're well enough paid already with all the things you've stolen while you worked here. It's lucky for you that I'd rather not trouble anyone to get them all back."

Mohammed replied, "Your stinginess now isn't worthy of a big man." Mohammed began to hide in the fields near Piero's house as often as he could, in hope to find a chance to get his money without being seen.

It happened that year in March that Ragnhild was to travel to Sumbawanga. Some time before she meant to leave, she said to Michael, "I've had several bad dreams about your staying behind. I'd rather you came with me instead."

"I've never weighed dreams as heavily as you do," answered the one-eyed man. "In any case, there's a good deal to keep me in the city just now."

Ragnhild replied, "No one likes to say evil of the future. Still, I fear we'll seem different to each other when I come home, if you won't do as I say."

Michael said, "It's as easy to be hurt on the roads as at home."

They left it at that, and Ragnhild left without him.

The moon was nearly full a week later. One white man and two black came to Michael's house in the night. They broke down the door.

Michael woke at the sound. He guessed what must be happening; he woke Signe and Edvard, and told them to hide. He himself went to face the thieves. They were already gathering up their new belongings when they saw Michael.

Michael grabbed the first man he could and clapped him twice in the face. The others closed on him with their knives drawn. Michael let the first man go and fell back to the doorway. He picked up one of his masks on the way and threw it. The mask hit one man on the head. They still came after him, however; two of them hit him with knives, one in the neck and one in the side. The second wound was Michael's death.

The thieves went through the house without fear and took whatever they liked. They found Signe in a closet from which she had seen her father die. They took her out and beat her, telling her to say nothing of what she had seen, if she meant to live longer. But the thieves did not find Edvard; he was under a bed that was too heavy to move. Despite the moonlight Edvard knew none of the men; Signe, on the other hand, had seen that the white man was Piero. The thieves left Michael's old house well laden.

The police came to Michael's house; Ragnhild came home from Sumbawanga. Everyone was agreed that Michael had been murdered. But the children said they knew none of the thieves; there were not enough traces otherwise to show who had struck Michael down. The police left without taking anyone with them.

Signe's Vengeance

Michael is the only one of his family to lie buried in Africa. His grave lies just north of Dar es Salaam. Zachias Mwakalinga gave a service for the American. Michael was put into the ground in a simple wooden box. But his friends sent a few of his favorite masks with him. Edvard put the first spadeful of earth into his father's grave; Signe said, "Father mine, a thousand thanks shall you have."

April and May are the time of the long rains in Dar es Salaam. The skies are often gray; the rain can last many hours at a time.

Signe made plans during the two weeks following Michael's death. She already knew where Piero lived. She found out how his rooms were laid out. She took Ragnhild's rat poison and found it had little taste and dissolved easily in water. She went over the way to Piero's house until she could walk it with her eyes closed.

The first rains came just before the new moon. Signe waited for a night that was both dark and stormy wet. She went by foot to Piero's about midnight. She saw no one because of the weather. Signe went into Piero's kitchen through a window. She took four bottles of beer, opened them and added poison to each. She saved the bottle tops and replaced them carefully; no one could easily see that they had been troubled. She recame home through the rain, and buried the poison bottle near a bridge on the way.

Signe could think that no one knew of her venture. In this, however, she was mistaken. Mohammed, the Arab who painted houses and who had a grudge against Piero, still spent his nights watching Piero's house. Already he had stolen some small things, but not so much as he thought right. He saw all that passed on this night, however, and followed Signe's path to see what might happen. He reached the creek in time to see Signe leave it empty-handed.

Piero saw that his kitchen floor was muddier than usual on the following morning. He thought little of the matter, however. Ragnhild also noticed the tracks in her kitchen. She asked Signe what she might know of them. Signe replied, "Nothing to speak of, but there might be some sore stomachs before long."

Piero recame home in the evening, and two friends with him. One was called Ismail and the other John. All three men took beer to drink. John said, "This tastes foul to my tongue, and it doesn't like my stomach much better." But he kept on drinking, nonetheless.

Ismail now said, "One could find better than this in any fishing village." He stopped drinking with that, but the others went on.

Soon all three men held their stomachs in pain. Neighbors answered their cries and went to find a doctor. The local healer would not leave his dinner to look after drunks, though, and it took some time for Piero and his friends to reach the sickhouse. By then Piero and John were very sick; they did not recover. But Ismail lived to tell what had happened.

Ragnhild found her poison missing on the day after the two men died. She asked Signe what she knew of this.

Signe replied, "I imagine it's gone to kill the man who killed Father." She went on to tell Ragnhild just what she had done, and then, "There shouldn't be any trouble in it, though; the rain must have washed out any signs."

"That's possible," said Ragnhild. "You've shown no wisdom in all this, in any case, especially when you make Edvard and me share the danger with you."

Ragnhild looked at her daughter a moment, and then went on, "I see you'd have tried this regardless. Since it's done, I'm not unhappy. But say nothing of the matter, not even to Edvard."

The police came a second time. Piero's neighbors said it was hard to understand the deaths. The man's mistress might have liked him dead, but she was gone from Dar es Salaam. The police learned that she had left even before Piero bought his beer. They looked in other places and found nothing to help them. After a time, they left off the search altogether; most of the neighbors did not seem very sorry at this outcome.

Mohammed came to Signe not many days later. He said, "I was no more fond of Piero than you were. That didn't make me kill him, though."

"I don't know what you mean," said Signe. "Beside, you say of me only what you hadn't the wit to pull off yourself."

"In any case," said Mohammed, "I've done you a favor not

to talk with the police of what I know. It's only right that you make good Piero's debt to me, since he can't pay it himself."

"Do you think me a fool?" asked Signe. "You'd have better luck with the dead man."

"In that case," said Mohammed, "I have nothing more to say to you for the moment. It's not likely that you've seen the last of me, though."

"'No man would live long if every threat bore fruit.'"

Ragnhild Moves Her Family

Signe and Edvard were not rowdy children in the best of times. They came more quiet still in the months after Michael died. Edvard spoke often with Zachias about Christ and the church; he did his best to avoid everyone else. Signe began to paint. Most her paintings show orange flowers against a blue sea and green fields. But there are sometimes three men bleeding by the side of a road.

Signe and Edvard returned to school in July. The other children saw that Signe acted strangely. They turned first from her and later from Edvard as well. Some called them witches and said they had been sent to undo the word of God which had freed Africa. Others said that Signe had only to look at food to poison it.

This last word pleased Ragnhild least of all.

Ragnhild spoke with Matthew and Zachias about the matter. Matthew said, "All people are brothers and sisters under heaven, or so it seems to me. But that's little seen between your children and the others. It's my guess they'll find only bad things as long as you stay in Michael's old house."

And Zachias the priest said, "White witches are worse than black, they say. There wasn't much to fear when the children spoke badly of Signe and Edvard only to each other. Now the parents fear your children as well, and tell theirs to keep a distance."

"You say no more than I've thought," said Ragnhild. "But I'm not free to move about when I'm tied to work here."

Matthew said, "You worked in Bagamoyo before. There must be other places as well."

"There is a sickhouse in Kigoma that could use me, I suppose; I have a friend there already."

Zachias said this seemed a fine idea. "We'll see if my friends in the government don't have something useful to say about it." Zachias thought a few moments and said, "It's not the best of years when one friend lies dead and others are about to leave. Still, there's no call to envy the dead." Ragnhild, Matthew, and Zachias drank beer together and talked of other days.

Ragnhild left Dar es Salaam before the Yule, and her family with her. They left some belongings with Zachias, in case they should someday return from Kigoma.

Welcome in Kigoma

Kigoma lies on the deepest lake in Africa, but it is far from the ocean, thirty-six hours by train. One goes first at night, through Morogoro and Kiosa, which are known for thieves. Mountains give way to flatland with the dawn, and one comes to Dodoma, where they make wine and have many important people to live. Flowers can be seen there, but the rest of the day is passed in dust, yellow and gray.

On the second morning, the sun rises over a river that flows into the Lake. It lies in a red land with many small trees and green plants. The train comes to rest in Kigoma soon after, at a great building next the water. The headlands around the town have no trees, but are alive with scraggle plants, as in our mountain lands. Yet the place is never cold.

• • •

Ragnhild went from the train in Kigoma to the house of Sara Mmari, her friend from the days of the Fenris sun in Morogoro. Sara lived south from the town and a bit away from the Lake. She had two daughters called Ann and Eunice, both younger than Edvard. Sara saw less of her children than she liked, but was counted the most gentle of mothers even so.

Sara's husband was used to drink. Some nights he beat her, and off and then the children as well. Sara sent him off after a time. He tried to come back to the house more than once, but Sara bought some bolts for the door. They were stout bars, and the husband stayed away after that. By the time Ragnhild reached Kigoma, he had moved elsewhere.

Sara knew from a letter why Ragnhild was come to the Deepest Lake. She said to the Norsewoman, "I had hoped to see you sooner and in better times."

Ragnhild answered, "I hoped that as well." But Sara would hear no more till she had fed the travelers breakfast.

Ragnhild now explained to her friend what had fallen them in Dar es Salaam and why they traveled so far.

Sara said, "I recall that I once promised you a roof if you needed it. It seems the time has come for you to hold me to my word." Sara gave Ragnhild and her children a room in her house. They stayed for three months, until they found a house of their own. After that, they lived in a village some way north of Kigoma.

Life on the Deepest Lake

There lies a town next to Kigoma and nearly as large called Ujiji. It was a slave market at one time. Later, the first Europeans in Africa met there; a large stone still marks the spot, graved with their names, a map of Africa, and a cross. Africans care little for the place, however.

Edvard often went to Ujiji, sometimes to the large stone, but most often to see a priest named Gregory Msuya. Gregory was a tall man, thirty years old, and not overburdened for followers.

He found a good deal of time for Ragnhild's son, young though he was.

Edvard also came to know Gregory's family, his mother and two brothers. One of these, named Augustine, lived with his wife and son and worked as a fisherman. But Edvard was most fond of the younger brother, who was called James. James was no more than twenty years old, but tall and well formed.

Edvard and James spent many days together doing one thing and another. Off and then it happened that they wandered far during the day. Then they would stay away and sleep under the sky.

One day they walked from Ujiji as usual. They followed a stream east from the Deep Lake. Near sunset they passed a village; it seemed a poor place. James led Edvard uphill from there until they came to a small glade. The two friends camped about halfway up the west side, where the morning light would strike first.

The night was a dark one, with no moon. Edvard lost little time falling asleep. But after a time, James rose and went down to the bottom of the glen. Other men soon came and joined James. They built a fire together. Most of the men formed a circle, and each one held a spear in one hand and an ostrich feather in the other. Three men stayed outside the circle to beat drums. A last man appeared, with a blindfold. He came up to the circle and danced to the drums. He took a spear from the first man he met. All the others chanted a verse, and the dancer exchanged the spear for an ostrich feather. This he did with each man in turn until, in the end, he had collected all the feathers to himself. Then he took off the blindfold and stood at the center of the circle, and laid the feathers around him so that one pointed to each man in the circle. All the others then bowed low to the man with the feathers.

Edvard wakened at the beginning of the dance and saw all that took place. Soon after the men bowed to their friend, the drums stopped and the fire smoldered out. All the dancers left the glen, save for James. He recame his sleeping place on the hillside.

• • •

At daybreak, Edvard asked his friend what was the point of all he had seen. James would say nothing at first, and then, "It would go badly for me if you knew too much about this."

But Edvard asked again, and James said, "Should I not help honor my cousin before he marries?"

Edvard replied, "I might have seen more if you had told me something sooner."

"Perhaps," said James. "Yet four generations of my family have been Christian, and still we don't see why the missionaries tried to take our drums. You're as white as they."

In those days, Edvard often asked James to come home with him to Kigoma. But for many months, James made one excuse or another and would not come. Once he said, "My mother doesn't trust any European far. We seem fine enough friends now, without upsetting her." But Edvard went right on asking his friend to join him.

At the last, James gave in and came. Things went well enough at first, and still better once James began to talk with Signe. By the end of the day, it seemed that he had no more doubts about visiting Edvard at home.

Once, when James had come to Edvard's house when Edvard was away, the European said, "It's a fine thing that you come more often, you who were once so shy. But I can hope you'll remember who was first your friend in this place."

James only laughed. He said, "It seems to me now that I can never have enough white friends, whatever my family chooses to think of it."

As for the rest of Ragnhild's family, Signe also went to Ujiji from time to time, but for her own reasons; she liked to paint the houses there. Some start at the ground with stone and turn to mud higher up. Others have cornerposts and windows of carved stone. But all are walled with mud and roofed with grass.

Ragnhild was soon a busy woman, watching the sick of Kigoma. She seldom had time to travel, even to so near a place as Ujiji. But she did watch for Sara's children off and then when their mother could not.

So things passed for more than two years. All the three, Ragnhild and her children, said they had looked never to see a time of peace last so long. Their neighbors came friends, and the shores of the Deepest Lake seemed the most welcoming in Africa. To eat fish all the year was a small price.

Of James and Mohammed

But the next years were hard ones for the lands beyond Kigoma. The rain failed more than once in Tanzania, and the head of the land was often ill. There came to be many thieves, even in the villages; in the cities they carried knives. More people than a few blamed the Europeans for all this.

Across the Deepest Lake, in Zaire, things were still worse. Bands of young men stole guns from the army. They went from one village to the next and took away whatever they liked.

After a time, the government of Zaire came tired of letting these bands do as they pleased. The bandits left behind only poor villages that could not be taxed. The government sent more of the army to the Lake; some of the young men stayed and fought jthe army in hope to gain more guns. But others thought it better to cross the Lake into Tanzania. There they raided in the countryside, and were soon joined by discontent Tanzanians.

All this began in the year when Signe was seventeen.

During this year also, James and Signe came to talk of marriage. Few other people liked the idea. James's brothers said nothing of the matter, and his mother said, "Edvard's not a bad child, but as for marriage, you must turn your face to see the world as it's coming to be. The future of the white people is dead and more than dead."

"White skin or black is no matter when people love each other as we do," said James. "You've nothing against Signe but her color, and that's not enough."

"You'll do well to think of what I say, even so."

Ragnhild was no better pleased. She thought Signe far too young a woman to think of wedding. When she said this, Signe replied, "We hope to live in Africa a long time; the sooner we make ourselves a part of it, the better."

Signe and James had wills of their own, in any event; it seemed most likely that the marriage would take place someday, though not perhaps within the year.

It happened once now that Signe walked into Kigoma, as she sometimes did. There and near the market she met Mohammed the Arab, that same Mohammed she knew from Dar es Salaam. He said, "I'm glad to see you after so long a time."

Signe replied, "I can't say the same. What brings you to this place?"

"I heard that you lived here now; I made it part of my studies to travel this way. I hoped to find you at home before long, but this is still better."

"I found our last meeting poor."

"We were both tired then," said Mohammed. "Now you must come with me and have a talk."

"No."

"Perhaps you've come shy. You should come to see me even so, unless you've forgotten all that I know of you."

Signe said, "You could prove nothing before; an evil tongue

gets no better hearing for years of being still."

"They say that the fear of witches can still the stoutest voice."

"Not yours, though."

"There's no reason for us to quarrel," said Mohammed. "I have a thing in my room to show you; you'll do better to see it than not."

Signe and Mohammed went together to the Arab's room. There was a bottle on the table next the bed. Mohammed said, "This bottle hid itself from me for a long time, though I looked for it often. I think you'll know it again, though; it's almost sure there's some trace of you on it still."

The bottle belonged to the poison Signe had used to kill Piero. She could see it was hers and said, "You can't think to get much hearing for such old charges, even with this to help."

"Perhaps you don't know that my father's come a judge. The family has more friends and mightier than before."

This was also a time when white faces were little welcome in the courts of Tanzania. Signe said, "What is it you ask of me?"

"You needn't fear for your money. I've enough now, and it's not right to beg from the poor. You do have another coin now, though, and in greater measure than before. I think it a fair price if you lie with me each day that I'm here. It's only a week, so some might count the price low."

Signe said, "I'll need a day to think on this. And you will have to give me the bottle at the end of the week, in case I do as you ask."

"I'm no miser," said Mohammed, "to quibble over a day for something that's waited years already. But if you stay from me, I won't be backward in pressing the case against you."

Signe left Mohammed after that. She went to talk with friends who knew about affairs of state. Everyone she talked with agreed that Mohammed's family was grown in power as he said. There was little good to be found in any argument with them.

Signe recame Mohammed's room the next day and did as he asked, and also for two days following. On the third afternoon, Mohammed fell asleep beside her. The Norsewoman saw this. She rose and dressed in silence, took the bottle from its table, and broke it against the wall. Mohammed woke at this sound. Signe turned to him and raked his face and chest with the broken bottleneck. Then she threw that too against the wall and broke it.

"You've given me something to remember," she said, "but I think you'll not soon forget me, either."

Signe was at the door by now. Mohammed was not yet fully risen. He said only, "You cut my face."

Signe left. But Mohammed was unclothed and had to stay behind. He went home to Dar es Salaam some few days later, and better marked than he had meant to be.

Signe's Firstborn

From this time Signe was pregnant. She did not wish a child. But Ragnhild refused to help stop the child herself; she said, "This is a thing you've fallen into on your own; now we'll all have to live with it."

And Sara Mmari told Signe that she could not trouble another doctor. "Many are the ways used to get at you Europeans these days."

After a time, it came clear to all that Signe waited a child. James came to see her. He said, "I see you've found further lovers than I."

Signe thought it unsafe to tell all of what had passed. She said only, "I can have no tears if you leave me over this; you can't have much use for me anyway, if you hope for things always to be proper."

James said, "This matter would strike any man badly. I've had only reasons to trust you up to now, though, so I'm of a mind to forgive what you've done and not to let it stand between us."

James went home and came back the next day. But now he said, "I can't see you anymore after your other lover's had you." He looked only at the window.

Signe said, "What's come of all your brave words from yesterday, if you say this now?"

"I've no wish to give you up for my own sake. But you and I have no way to care even for a child of our own, let alone someone else's. Anyway, I can't defy my mother so far. One chooses a wife as one likes, but never comes free from a mother and her family."

Edvard spoke little with Signe in these months. He spent most his nights in Ujiji. Once he did say to Ragnhild, "I don't know how I've stayed so long in a house with a sister like Signe. It's bad enough that she steals my friends, but then she can't be troubled to stick by them afterwards."

Ragnhild said, "Signe's not always wise, but she's your sister all the same, and a brave one at that."

The time came for Signe to give birth. She stayed at home with only Ragnhild and a midwife beside her. Edvard stayed away in Ujiji. Signe gave birth to a son; it seemed born to good health. But at night, after the midwife left, it left off breathing and died before morning.

Ragnhild told her daughter, "You had a lot of worry for something so little lasting."

"It's true my life hasn't often come so easily on its own," said Signe.

Signe's baby was not the first to die in the village. It was buried, as was the custom with some tribes, as soon as possible and in an unmarked grave, so to keep the child's spirit from plaguing people.

Not long after this, James came to see Signe. He said, "I never wanted to leave you in the first place. Now that God's forgiven you, there's nothing that can keep us apart, even if my mother says something else." He said a number of other things, all of them friendly.

Signe listened to James till he finished. Then she said, "You're the sweetest lad I know to think so well of me. Still, I think you'll never listen to me over your mother; we'll do best to keep ourselves apart." James talked with Signe some time longer, but she would not change her mind. He went home after that and did not visit Kigoma again for many months.

Edvard's Dream

At about this time, there came reports to Kigoma that the Zairians and their hangers-on were coming bolder, striking in daylight and moving closer to the towns. Gunshots could be heard off and then at night, even in Kigoma itself.

Sara came to Ragnhild's house. She said, "I think you've heard the rumors and also the shooting."

"I'm not deaf as yet," said Ragnhild.

"I think you should take them to heart and leave this place as soon as you can."

"You speak only what's prudent," said Ragnhild. "But it's all too easy for us to spend our whole lives going up one road and down the next in search of a safe place. I don't think we can afford to leave at each sound of danger."

"You're well enough warned now," said Sara. "But I think you're like to find yourselves in a bad way before long. Then you must come to my house and see if we can't keep you alive, anyway."

Ragnhild thanked her friend for her kindness. But Sara Mmari said, "I fear you're as proud even as I."

Edvard still went to Ujiji, though he stayed there overnight less often. He had forgiven Signe her sins and often talked with her now.

One day Edvard came to the white man's rock in Ujiji. By this time he had been to the spot often enough that people thought nothing of seeing him there. He sat at the base of the map rock to think, but fell asleep instead.

Afterward, Edvard told Signe this dream: "It seemed to me that I walked in a valley of Konde carvings. Each was made from a tree, and higher than a man's head. No path lay before me, and however I went, the carvings curled more frightening. At last I came on a tree, a baobab and larger than any other. There was a door carved in it in the form of a cross. I knew it was the way to my salvation. In front the door sat a key-clad elf. He said, 'Your forelders kept me hidden from God one time. Now I'll save Him the trouble of seeing you.' Nothing I did would get the key from him.

"Soon there came a woman. I saw from her feet that she must be you. This woman whispered something to the elf. He threw down the key and ran off into the forest of carvings. The woman unlocked the door of the tree. I went inside, but she stayed behind. The door closed, and that's the last I saw of her."

Signe said, "It takes no seer to say that this dream promises you my help to get to your heaven. Still, I doubt you'll get me to push you to your Christ, the lord of simpers."

There Edvard let the matter lie.

Revolt

The gunshots came nearer and more frequent in the weeks following. In August, Ragnhild agreed that the danger was too great to stay on. She planned to leave in three days' time.

Edvard went to bid farewell to Gregory Msuya the priest and his family. He came first to the church, and talked with Gregory for some time.

Just after noon; they heard loud voices and many from the southern part of the town. They came outside the church. There were several fires in the town already, and many people running through the streets. They could guess easily enough that the rebels were come and meant to take all Ujiji in a short time.

"They've come sooner than is good for anyone," said Gregory, "and it's worst for you. I can't keep you safe even in the church, if these men are as bad as people say." Gregory and Edvard went instead to the house of Gregory's brother Augustine, the fisherman. Augustine had already decided to take his family out on the Lake; he did not want them to face the risk of staying at home. He agreed to take Edvard as well.

Augustine hid Edvard in the bottom of his boat, underneath his fishing nets. In this way the family could be friendly with other boatmen who would not like a white face. They traveled south for three days, eating very little.

The news soon reached Kigoma of what had fallen Ujiji. Ragnhild feared for Edvard, but there was nothing to be done. She and Signe went instead to Sara's house. Ragnhild told her friend, "Your advice before was better than I would admit. You'll have good reason to refuse us now, since I didn't listen to you then. Still, I hope you won't forsake us."

Sara answered, "I like my life better than to send a friend to death." She led her guests to a space under the kitchen; it was a small place, damp and rat-ridden. Ragnhild and Signe had no complaint about it, though.

The rebels came to Kigoma late in the afternoon. They went into every house and took whatever pleased them. When someone chanced to annoy them, they killed the person, or else burned the house. The sky shone red from their fires after dark.

The rebels had least mercy in places where Europeans or officials lived. They shot each person they found in such a house.

The rebels came to Sara's house only once in the beginning; she was not important enough to waste time on. The soldiers did not refuse to take her pots and clothes, though.

On the day following, the rebels gathered in the marketplace; they feasted their victory from morning to night. Many local people joined them, some from fear of being thought unfriendly, others because they liked the rebels better than the government.

A group of rebels recame Sara's house on the third day. They had heard that she was friendly with some Europeans and thought she might harbor them still. Sara had moved her guests to a place between the ceiling and the roof by this time; they could be better hidden behind piles of bottles and sacks.

The soldiers were much more thorough than on the first day. They found the place under the kitchen and marked the remains of people there. Sara said that her children were in the habit to play there, though she told them not to. They also found the attic. But the smell of poison was strong there; anyone could see that the place held nothing more than Sara's work things. They held on asking questions some time longer, but they could find nothing and had to leave.

There were flashes of light to be seen in the sky soon after nightfall, and heavy sounds shook the ground. Cannon tore away at the city through the night. By morning, all the rebels were gone; the government's soldiers walked in to take their place. They were not gentle with those they met.

The army soon found who were the people who had feasted with the rebels. They brought ten of these to the marketplace just at noon and shot them dead. They took many others to a small

camp beside their own. These people went later to the police in
Dar es Salaam.

Ragnhild and Signe were among six Europeans who lived
through the battles in Kigoma and Ujiji. They came out from
their hiding places when the army came. The government had
no wish to keep them in so dangerous a place and told them to
leave within three days.

Ragnhild did not like to go. She feared for Edvard no less
than on the first day, and told her fears to Signe. The daughter
replied, "He's too much trouble to disappear so easily." But she
also told Ragnhild of Edvard's dream.

Ragnhild said, "We're bound to see him again, if dreams have
power; I'm sure you've not helped him on that path up to now."

Ragnhild's voice was not strong as she spoke in this way; still,
there was no choice but to leave Kigoma, as things stood.

Signe Finds Work

Signe and Ragnhild recame Dar es Salaam. The government still
paid Ragnhild and gave her a house, though she had little work
to do. Ragnhild asked Signe to stay with her. But Signe said,
"That seems to me a poor idea, since I'm a grown woman now."
She stayed instead in a hut near the ocean. The hut belonged to
Matthew Basumingera.

At about this time, the head of Tanzania died. It had been his
idea to welcome Europeans who wished to work for the nation
in the first years after Ragnarok. Later, he stopped the country
from sending the whites away, though there were those who
hoped to send the milkears away to their own profit.

The new head listened to different voices. He decided to help
the Europeans leave whenever possible, and told the police to

study all the whites they could with an eye to finding crimes they could be accused of. Generally, when the police found something amiss, they offered the Europeans a choice: to take the chance of a trial, or to leave Tanzania with most of their belongings intact. Few chose to stay on such terms.

In the months after recoming Dar es Salaam, Signe sought work. She could find no better job, however, than to paint a house that belonged to Zachias the priest. She took as long as she could at this; it seemed little likely she would find anyone else willing to go far to help a European.

Edvard Returns

So things held on until December. Then one day, Edvard came to Dar es Salaam and on to Signe's place. He was much thinner and darker of skin than when the family had parted.

Signe sent word at once to Ragnhild to say that Edvard was safe with her and to ask her to join them. Signe gave Edvard a meal; Ragnhild came just when Edvard finished eating. Mother and son held on to each other for some time, and laughed to be together once more.

Now Edvard spoke of his travels on leaving Kigoma, and told this story:

"Three days we fared south in the boat, and I spent most of the time in the bottom, wet and coming bone-weary. We put to shore in a land that was poor and rough. The few farmed fields couldn't keep their furrows straight, and the people were little used to strangers. Augustine and his family soon put out to the Lake again, but I stayed behind, since there seemed little point to recome Kigoma.

"I slept the first night in the open. Then I took the path inland in hopes to leave the Lake far behind. Most the day I walked and came only to other poor places. The women could do no better than to wear dark blue tatters when they could afford that, and I saw few grown men. The huts were meager; I heard a single radio and saw no wrist clocks at all.

"At last, I came very hungry and to a village that seemed a bit better off than most. They had lanterns there and a flag. I talked with some the people; finally one of them, a woman called Salama, offered me food and a sleeping place, if I would help her with her fieldwork. She said, 'It's a poor offer when I can't give you any money for your work. But you'll find there aren't many coins in the whole of the town, and those have passed from hand to hand so often that they've come quite smooth.'

"Things were not quite so bad there as she said, I think. Still, I had to accept her offer. I worked long days for a week and two days more. The sun was not too hot, but as fierce to the eyes as I can remember. It drove me dizzy more than once. Salama gave me maize meal for food and let me bring us both water from the well. Sometimes we had fire and sometimes not.

"I was quite weak by the time of my second Sunday in the place. But by then I heard of a church in another village eight kilometers away. I told Salama that everyone had need of God, and that she must give me leave to go to church of a Sunday. She agreed to this at last, from fear that I might leave otherwise. That Sunday I left early in the morning, but could not walk the whole way to God's house. Instead, I took some sleep by the roadside before going back to Salama. But I told her the service had been a fine one.

"Work was just as hard in the weeks following, and the food no better. But I gained enough strength to get all the way to church on Sundays. The church itself was partly new and partly old. The steeple was small and still in scaffolding, but the main roof leaked from lack of repair. The pastor seemed a nice sort of man. After some weeks, I came to talk with him. At last I told him how I came there, and that I hoped somehow to find my family once more.

"He said, 'It's difficult when you don't know where to go,

even if you found a way to leave this land.'

"I agreed that this was so. In the end, the pastor gave me paper for a letter to Gregory to ask where you were. He posted it for me as well. It happened too that the bishop was coming in two weeks' time and might be able to help me.

"After that I went to church every Sunday, religiously, as they say, in hope to get some answer to my letter and prayers, and as well to get away from Salama. But no letter came on the first Sunday or on the one following. The bishop did come; he said I might ride with him away from that part of the country, but there was no reason in it when I had nowhere to go.

"It was only some weeks later that I had word from Gregory to say where you and Mother had gone, and another month or more before the bishop recame the place. All this time Salama used my help for all she could and then some. She grew fatter with each day, and I thinner.

"When the bishop came back, I told him where the two of you had gone. He said that he didn't often come to Dar es Salaam, but that he would take me to his house some miles from Singida. We rode together five full days to reach his house; I stayed there with the bishop's family for another week, and could think myself in good health once more.

"Then the bishop took me down to Singida and bought me a ticket on the bus to Dar es Salaam. I thanked him as best I could; he left me to find the way.

"There is a bus from Singida to Dar es Salaam every day. It starts from Mwanza. But they let no one on if the bus is too crowded already, so that one can wait a long time to get a place. There were about a hundred people who waited buses to one place and another when I got there. We lay under an open shelter at night and talked or played dice through the day.

"Singida is a cold place at this time of year, especially at night. On my second night there, I came chilled through my shirt. A man who lay nearby soon noticed me. He took off his blanket and put it over me. Then he shared the blanket of a friend. We couldn't talk, though, because he knew no Swahili.

"Even with that, I sickened once more. All the day following, I had fever and chills. Finally, in the evening, I found a place on the bus. We traveled through the night and came to Dar es Salaam this noon. But as you can see, I'm still weak and tremble-fingered. It was all I could do to find my way out to this place where you live."

And indeed it was true that Edvard could barely hold his teacup without spilling it. Signe and Ragnhild let him to say no more, but put him to bed.

In the morning, Ragnhild and Signe told Edvard of their own adventures. At the last, Ragnhild asked her son if he had any plans for the future.

Edvard replied that he hadn't thought on the matter as yet.

Signe then said, "I think you should stay here to rest as long as need be. After that, you could help me to work on this house if you like."

Edvard agreed to this and said, "It will be a new thing to do work I choose, and to be paid for it into the bargain."

Ragnhild's Family Meet the Police

Early in the year following, Zachias sold the house that Signe had kept herself busy by painting. Many people then heard of her work. Among them was Mohammed. He also heard that she had no child with her, though she had been pregnant before. He asked some of his friends what was known of this. They said that nothing was certain, but that many whispers had it that Signe had killed her own.

Mohammed came to Signe and said, "You've made an enemy of me who might have been a friend. I'm as slow to forget that as you hoped."

"You're slow of many things, if you only now come to see me."

Mohammed went to the police and told them all the rumors he knew about Signe Ragnhilds-datter.

A policeman came to Signe's house not many days later. He told her, "You have been charged with killing an infant."

"You can't think to hold me on so slim and ugly a rumor," said she.

The policeman replied, "It's not for you to say what can be done and what not." He bound her hands and took her off to prison.

Later in the same day, another policeman came to Edvard. He was a well-fed man of high rank. He said, "I don't know the truth of the charge against your sister, and it's likely you don't, either. Whatever happens, she stands in danger from the case. But to get the evidence against her might be costly for us."

Edvard agreed that Signe wouldn't be caught easily.

"Still," said he, "you'd hardly have come so far just to say that."

"We're not in the habit to bargain with human lives," said the policeman, "nor to show kindness to criminals. But I can tell you this, that we won't have to press the case against Signe, if you get her, your mother, and yourself out of the country."

"That's most kind of you. When must we leave?"

"That's a hard thing to know surely. But I'd guess that if Signe's not gone within the month, she'll come to trial. Once she's before the court, nothing will stop them."

"This isn't the easiest of choices you offer me," said Edvard.

"I don't offer choices; I only tell you things you might find useful."

• • •

Edvard went first to see Zachias the priest, who lived on the way to Ragnhild's. He told the priest what had fallen Signe and said, "I'm not sure what to do now, since the matter is so little of my own making."

Zachias answered, "You're not the first person to have burdens you don't like. If Signe's done what they say, there's little good to be said of her. But it's best for a brother not to try too hard to find the truth of matters; others will like that work better."

Edvard thought for a moment and said, "They ask a lot of us to leave the only land we know."

"If you think of yourself, Edvard, you've always wanted to be a child of God. All the earth is His as much as this land you've seen up to now."

Zachias also said that he had a friend called Christian Maeda. This man was a captain for a ship that sailed from Dar es Salaam to the Azores and on to America.

Edvard went to Ragnhild and told her what he knew. She said, "We must surely get Signe out of this land; she's too daring for anyone's good. Then we'll have it to choose to follow or not, though it's not a choice I'd have chosen."

"No more would I," said Edvard. "But we must all go if one goes. The people who hate Signe today won't fail to hate you or me tomorrow."

Mother and son went to see Captain Maeda. The captain was a slim man, handsome of face, with yellow teeth and missing half an ear; no one marked it, though, that he heard any the less well for that. His ship was called the *Kasuku;* it had a brightly colored bird on its prow, and was a ship versed in seas and ports past number. Captain Maeda himself seldom had much use for Europeans, but he agreed to let the Norse family sail with him.

Ragnhild and Edvard made everything ready. All their belongings were on board when Signe came free from jail the day before the *Kasuku* sailed. The whole family stayed in a single cabin.

Zachias Mwakalinga and Matthew Basumingera came to the ship just before it sailed. Zachias gave Edvard a blanket made of rich wool and woven with a difficult design. The priest said, "You've made the best choice. We're not like to see each the other again, but you shouldn't think I'll soon forget you, either."

Edvard took the blanket, held it to his face, and kissed it, but he could find nothing to say.

Matthew spoke mostly to Ragnhild and Signe. He said he had nothing to give them; he did not expect to live in freedom much longer. "But," said he, "I think we've meant a lot to each other, and will in times to come, somehow or other."

Zachias and Matthew left the *Kasuku* soon after, and the ship weighed anchor to sail from Dar es Salaam.

Ocean Journey

The passengers ate together on the ship, and often with members of the crew, or even with the captain. Captain Maeda had little patience for Edvard's talk of God, but he came fond of Signe and Ragnhild because they spoke more of practical things.

Ragnhild and her children decided where they would live after leaving Africa. Ragnhild chose to go to Norway, since that was her land from before the war, and she had few ties to any other. But Signe meant to go on to America; she could not rest without having seen her father's home in Wisconsin. Edvard also decided to go to America, in hopes to find a place he could think his own.

The *Kasuku* came to the Azores after a month's time. Some say that these islands take their name from the color of the seas around them. However that is, many people come to the Azores; Africans find in them a place by the sea and cooler than they are customed to; Europeans hope to escape the hunger and fighting that visit many houses at home.

Ragnhild took her leave of Signe and Edvard in the Azores. She said, "None of us knows what the future's like to hold. Let us agree on one thing, that each will help the others in time of need, whatever else may happen between now and then."

Edvard and Signe had no difficulty to agree to that.

Then Signe said, "We also have a good deal of baggage, we three. But you'll be settled sooner than we, Mother, so I think it's best for you to take everything, save the nearest things we'll need in America."

Edvard agreed and said, "We're more likely to come home to you than the other way around, in any case."

Ragnhild left the ship soon after and took all the things they asked with her. But Signe and Edvard stayed on the *Kasuku* and sailed on till they reached Louisiana early in August. Signe then told Captain Maeda of their plan to go on to Wisconsin, and asked if he knew of anything that might help them on their way.

The captain replied, "You're foolish to travel so far in a land you know nothing of. You're not like to find any better a life in Wisconsin than here in the south, either."

But he could see that they meant to go north regardless.

Later in the day, Captain Maeda spoke with some men he knew in Louisiana. In the evening, he called Signe and Edvard into his cabin and said, "Even if you must go north, there's no need to go alone." He gave them the name of a woman called Olivia, whom he had heard also wished to reach Wisconsin.

Signe and Edvard thanked the captain for his trouble on their behalf. They left the *Kasuku* in the morning, the second that the ship stayed in port in Louisiana, which the Spanics call Novo Brasil.

❄ Part Two
America

Introduction

North America in the years between 20 and 30 M. E. was still a land ravaged by war. A small population (in prewar terms) lived mostly from subsistence agriculture; small industries existed only for the domestic market, and then to make a bare handful of products. Transportation networks functioned only intermittently, and at a minuscule fraction of the rate of prewar times—but the presence of outside powers guaranteed a small flow of oil and spare machine parts.

Politically, North America fell under the sway of its neighbors to the south, in the first instance of Brasil and Mexico; later of Venezuela, Chile, and Argentina as well. Generally, each of the powers took those lands that were most convenient to it and richest in the remains of prewar times. Many parts of the continent that were difficult to reach, or that had little to offer, were left outside the control of any Latin power. Such was the case for the rich but heavily bombed eastern seaboard, and for the Pacific northwest.

Of the two powers mentioned in *Signe's Saying* (Brasil and Argentina), Brasil was far the more hated. The Brasilians attempted to control every facet of life in Novo Brasil and sent a small army of functionaries to enforce their will. Both the functionaries and the real army sent to bolster their authority were greatly resented by the local people.

The Argentines, on the other hand, used local powers as far as possible. On most occasions, they even preferred to use North American mercenary soldiers than to send their own armed forces.

Local governments of this period varied widely in form. But all faced a common problem in the antagonism between large farmers (who tended to gather great estates around them) and small freeholders or tenants (whose numbers grew throughout the period). Many local authorities descended into barbaric cruelty because of the demands placed upon them. Most were religious in character, in part because the devastation loosed a general religious revival, and in part because few could muster the force needed to rule without a pretense of divine sanction.

Olivia

It is said that the first from Europe to find America was a Norseman named Leif. Later, many others came, and there are not now many Norse among the Americans.

Signe and Edvard sought out that Olivia of whom Captain Maeda had told them. She was an Easterner, a thin woman, shorter than most, with large ears and dark hair. She looked neither strong nor quick, but could be both.

Olivia had come to Louisiana in the seventh year before Signe and Edvard left Africa. This was thought a great honor at the time; few from the east are let to live in the rest of America. They are thought unlucky and their voices odd. Olivia never found herself fully happy in Novo Brasil, even so. One day in the third summer she stayed there, she found a friend called Kieth, also an Easterman, kneeling before a Spanic statue and kissing its foot. She kicked him into the statue and broke it; the Brasilians put her in jail for that.

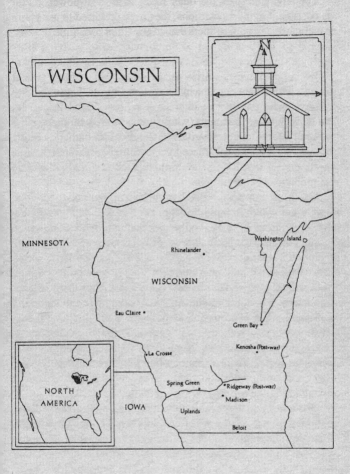

• • •

Olivia had been free for some weeks when Signe and Edvard arrived in America. She had no stomach to recome the east, however, and thought to travel north in hope to find her brother, a man called Stephen. Olivia had heard that he was well placed under the Argentines, at a place called Spring Green, on the Wisconsin River.

Olivia, Edvard, and Signe soon came to be friends. They sailed together up the Great River for eight days, till they reached a village called Hickman. There they left the river, because it soon meets the Eastern River; the meeting place is so unhealthy that even boatman bring no jokes of it.

The three travelers walked from Hickman instead, for four weeks and two days in all. Most of the land they saw was flatter than any part of Norway, and so rich that corn grew even where it was not planted. Near the end of the journey, in Wisconsin, there were more of both hills and cows, and as well some lakes, as in Sweden.

Signe, Edvard, and Olivia now came on a shallow river, whose banks were flat and covered with small rocks. Olivia thought that this must be the Wisconsin; they followed it downstream for two days, until they reached Spring Green. There are many strange houses in that place; they seem to grow from the ground like plants or rocks. There is also an odd grave, marked only by a large and uncarved stone, with small stones set into a circle roundabout. No one knows who is buried in it, or why so far from the town's churchyards. Most think it a holy spot from the old days; some call it Spirit Rock and say it brings the warmth for an early spring.

Stephen the Nearly Lucky

Olivia's brother Stephen had lived at Spring Green for three years at this time. He was a thin man and thoughtful, a soldier with black hair and deeply set eyes. In later years he came to write books as well as to fight. In time also, he came something of a champion to the poor and was called the Nearly Lucky, because people were seldom able to keep all that he won for them.

Even before Olivia left the east to come to Novo Brasil, Stephen was a soldier. He fought with anyone who paid him and served in several places, particularly against the French in Canada. It is said he fought mostly for plunder in those years. In any case, he showed himself a brave and clever man, as useful in speaking with an enemy as in fighting him.

Most of the eastern soldiers recame home after the wars in Canada ended, in the hope of finding a use for their spoils. But Stephen did not want to live in the east; he thought it a land of death. He thought as well that it would be wasteful to stop fighting when he was still so young, and he set about to find a new place for himself.

This was the time when the Argentines began to rule in Wisconsin, which they called Bolivar. They thought it too expensive to send an army of their own to conquer the land, or a government to run it; they made a treaty instead with the Church of the Second Rebirth, which was then quite strong in Wisconsin. This church holds that God sent the war as a way to bring new life to the world.

The treaty let the church to rule the land for the Argentines, provided that it sent a part of its tithes each year to Buenos Aires and traded with no one else beside the Argentines. In turn, Argentina promised to buy soldiers to help bring the Lord's word to those who had had trouble hearing it so far.

Stephen was among the captains the Argentines hired to come to Wisconsin. He brought a few lieutenants with him, but had to find most of his soldiers in Wisconsin itself. He found this difficult to do at first; most people in Wisconsin would not lightly trust an outlander. Two soldier captains died for their trouble, and others soon left without having done anything of value.

But Stephen was a stubborn man; he learned to show people the sides of the church they would like best—its promise that villages might live in peace, and the chance to sell cheese and grain in distant markets. Stephen fought with skill and growing fortune; in time he came to be the best-famed captain in Wisconsin.

When the fighting ended, Stephen thought to marry the eldest daughter of the Bishop John of Ridgeway. He hoped in this way to make his place in Wisconsin a lasting one, for he no longer wished to go from one country to the next with his rifle for company.

The bishop opposed the marriage at first. He said that soldiers were no better than thieves. But the church fathers in Kenosha had no wish to lose a man like Stephen. They promised John more fee-paying lawsuits to hear; after a time, the bishop gave way. But he never forgot his doubts entirely. He said, "I've three more daughters at home, and each one prettier than this."

John's daughter, Stephen's wife, was named Minna; she was as dark of hair as Stephen, proud and tall without shoes, known for being both farseeing and prudent. She wanted a husband to be the match for her father and his place in things; she and Stephen got on well at first. Their yard at Spring Green was a gift of the church and in keeping with the debt owed to Stephen's triumphs.

God-fearers and Bloodhands

There were many quarrels in Wisconsin in those years, even when the church was at its strongest. The most common dispute was over tithes and the claim by tenants that the rate should be lower when crops were poor. Some people in the church said that the tithes were set by God and sealed in blood at each village, and must stay the same in all years. These people called themselves

God-fearers and were the owners of land as often as not.

Their enemies were called bloodhands, after the time that one of them, a priest called Mark, cut his own wrist at a meeting of the Church Council and said, "If the poor must bleed for you, then I shall bleed for them." The bloodhands said that the landlords brought great hardship on the land when they took as great a share of the crop in bad years as in good. They feared also that hunger might make tenants unrestful.

The church fathers were never willing to stand entirely with one side or the other in these arguments, but instead helped first the God-fearers and then the bloodhands. It was said they feared that landlords and tenants might come to hate each the other for all time, if either side had its way too far.

The summer was cool and the harvest poorer than usual in the year before Signe and Edvard came to America. Many landlords looked to have less money than they thought they needed, especially in the north where the sun was weakest. The God-fearers came to argue that, if anything, the tithe rates ought to be raised rather than lowered. The bloodhands came even less happy with their opponents than usual.

In the end, the bloodhands carried the church fathers with them, and the tithes were unchanged, in part because the Primate himself stood against the God-fearers. The council also sent four of the loudest of the God-fearing priests off to live on Washington Island, a windswept and bitter land in the middle of Michigan Lake. But the council agreed too to let the four priests to try their ideas on the island, if they wished.

No one thought the matter finally settled by these measures, and the dispute between God-fearers and bloodhands was still hotly debated in many places, even between brothers. Bishop John, Minna's father, was a God-fearer, and took that side whenever he came to Spring Green. He said that the Argentines wanted their due as much in bad years as in good, and that it seemed to him a sacrilege for the church of God to be stinted and the best people in the land made to suffer, when everyone else came off well.

But most of Stephen's soldiers had been tenants; he was not the man to forget them just because peace had come. He told his father-in-law that if God wanted His full share, He must send rain.

The two men talked to this end more than once before John said that the marriage vows of a blasphemer meant nothing. He stopped from coming to Spring Green and wrote letters to Minna urging her to leave as well. But there was little more he could do; the church fathers still stood with Stephen.

As for Minna, she was much torn. She trusted the chances of neither husband nor father, yet neither would stand down from speaking just as he saw fit. She was apt to come short of temper when she thought much on the matter.

Olivia's Reception in Spring Green

Edvard, Signe, and Olivia came at last to a church and a hall which stood on the north bank of the river. Both church and hall are built up to let the river flood the basements in springtime. They stand some way south from the village of Spring Green itself.

Minna met them at the door and asked, "Who are you to be wandering about while everyone else works?"

Olivia gave her name and said, "I am Stephen's sister, and I think he'll see me, though we've been many years apart. These are friends of mine from Africa. They seek their father's old house in Madison."

Minna said, "'Who claims Madison for a home is a dead man.'" She looked more closely at Olivia and said, "I see that you might have something of Stephen's eyes—though many others could say the same. You'll have to be welcome here, at least until he sees you."

A serving man led the travelers inside the hall and into a small room to one side. He brought them porridge and water, but otherwise left them alone. They could do no more than listen to the cows outside till evening came.

Stephen came to see his guests at sundown and saw that it was indeed his sister whom he met, though she was thinner and darker-skinned than before. Brother and sister held each other a long time in greeting.

Stephen now asked Olivia if she had found all the comfort she hoped for in Wisconsin.

"It's as good as can be hoped," said Olivia, "when there's only a single room to spare and little food."

"What do you say?" asked Stephen. "There's more than enough of everything here."

"Then it must be the custom here to serve guests no more than porridge and water during the day. Still, there aren't many places where it's an honor to be locked up."

Stephen asked Minna if it were true that his guests had fared so badly. She said it was, "because we can't be lavish with everyone who says he knows you."

Stephen made no reply to that, but led all three of his guests down to the main hall. He had ale brought for them, and a large meal. Olivia came more cheerful as she ate; soon she borrowed an old flute from Stephen and played it while the others drank their ale.

In the morning Stephen said, "I hope for all three of you to stay the winter here, and not to go wandering off."

Olivia agreed at once. But Signe only thanked Stephen for his offer and said that she and Edvard meant to go on to Madison as soon as they could.

Stephen laughed at this and said, "That'll be in the spring, anyway. It's an empty place now with neither food nor roof for you."

Edvard seemed doubtful still, and Signe said that they would stay only if Stephen let them pay for the trouble they would bring. But Stephen said the church did not take money from those in need. "If you must give us something, speak freely of the lands you've seen. We seldom hear of the wide world." Signe and Edvard gave in after that and said they would stay.

These arrangements did not please Minna. She told Stephen, "You've a duty to Olivia, and no one will grudge it that you give her a place. But as for these others, wisdom's a better thing than kindness. You know nothing of them; at the best, people will say we've wasted our trust on worthless people. That sort of talk will only bring you trouble, when you have enough already."

Stephen replied, "They're my sister's friends; I wouldn't think much of a god that made me throw Africans to the snow, either."

"They're no more Africans than I am," said Minna.

"What's done has to be lived with, in any case."

There is little to tell of the winter following until after Yule; but it seemed that Stephen and Signe were more than a little fond one for the other, and also that Edvard was restless.

Stephen Raids Washington Island

News came to Spring Green early in the new year that the small farmers of Washington Island had laid hold of all their churchmen and refused to pay their tithes for the following year. There was also a message for Stephen from the church fathers in Kenosha. It read:

Hail Stephen, soldier of the faith,

We are minded of your great prowess and manifold virtues, and pray you to consider a journey to quell the rebels of Washington Island.

It seems likely that these islanders resent their new priests. Their anger may lend them strength, for it seems they do not remember that a bad priest is still better than none at all.

We feel certain that the sooner these islanders are given peace, the better it will show the folly of denying God's will. Therefore, we authorize you, Stephen, captain by the order of this Council and by the Grace of God, to raise what troops you like and to proceed to Washington Island, as soon as it may suit you. We give our solemn word to pay a soldier's wage and a half to as many as one hundred men in your company.

With faith that your resolve will equal your reverence, as it has in the past, we remain,

The Guardian Council of the Second Rebirth.

Minna was a woman of some wisdom; she liked this venture no better than she did her winter guests. She said, "They give you so few men that you could easily lose. And if you don't, people will only think of you more, when it's wisest not to be seen at all."

Stephen replied, "I can't refuse the church what it asks; it's given me all I have, and it's done the same for you."

Stephen raised the men he wanted easily enough from his old company. They marched to the headland facing Washington Island at the end of January. The priest of the headland church gave them a boat to cross the lake and a pilot to guide the way. But he also said, "This crossing's called Death's Door. The ice is bad now, and the current's sunk good ships even in the summer."

Stephen replied, "Perhaps we're meant to live through it even so. Or if not, we'll go to death blessed by God."

In the event, the crossing was a quiet one.

Washington Island is a small place, almost square, several kilometers on a side. Its farmers are poor, but customed to do things in their own way. They trust to the lake to protect them.

The islanders saw Stephen's boat as it came in. Many of them came down to the dock to meet her. More than a few were armed.

But neither Stephen nor the islanders were eager to fight. One of the islanders talked with Stephen for a few minutes. Then the islanders gave the soldiers a theater hall to use as a barracks, provided they carried no weapons in public.

Each day for the next week, Stephen met with the island's council, five men who had been chosen by the rest to speak for all. Everything went in a friendly enough way, though there were no agreements reached. At last Stephen told the councillors he meant to recome Kenosha and explain all they had told him to the church fathers. These words cheered the islanders; they had feared worse.

Stephen now asked the council to join him for dinner and to bring their families. The islanders would not come till Stephen agreed to send all his men back to their ship, so there could be no ambush.

All through the feast day, Stephen sent soldiers back and forth to the docks in the guise of loading aboard all they had brought to the island. But in the confusion, he hid eight men in the rafters of a storeroom, which lay to the right and behind the stage.

At the end of dinner and before dessert, the eight men came out and laid hold of all the islanders. Stephen asked the councillors to have the four God-fearing priests brought to him. This was done; the islanders feared for themselves and for their families.

Stephen took both the priests and the families down to his ship, and in the morning he sailed back to the mainland. But he let the families recome home with the promise that the islanders would get the same mercy from the church that the priests did. Stephen promised also to say that he thought the tithes on the island should be returned to their former levels.

Stephen brought the priests and councillors to Kenosha; then he and his men fared westward home.

Signe and Edvard Part

Spring now came, and all new things with it. Stephen was by now so pleased with his guests that he did not want them to leave. He found an empty farm for Olivia to stay on, and he told Signe of a shop in Spring Green. "The man who owns it saw his wife die two years ago," said Stephen. "They say he drinks a lot since then, but in any case, he's no match for the store." Stephen thought Signe could have the shop, if she wished.

Olivia went out to her farm as soon as the snow melted. But Signe said nothing in reply for the time being; she still hoped to live in Madison, as her father had.

Signe and Edvard traveled to the ruins of Madison in the middle of the spring. Around the city and in all directions are several kilometers of buildings, broken and mostly black from fire. Nonetheless, Madison grieved less from the war than did many other places; one could walk right to the middle of it, even in those days.

No people lived in the city, though, and Ragnhild's children met no one. They did see the four lakes of which Michael had spoken highly. But the trees he said greened the city to summer were gone; the thin ones growing new would not hide the remaining walls even in August, nor would vines look them whole.

• • •

Edvard said, "Father didn't miss much by being in Africa, whatever he thought."

"No," said Signe, "though living long isn't the only thing."

"No one lives here now, long or short," said Edvard. "And I hardly think it will do for us. Still, one can like the quiet." There was not even the sound of a bird in the city.

Edvard and Signe recame their camp west of the city at nightfall. Signe said to Edvard, "I think we might do best to take that shop Stephen speaks of and run it together."

Edvard said, "It's bad enough that you raid a marriage bed; but worse that you choose a man who likes to kill anyone he can't fool."

"I never looked to have a dung beetle for a brother, Edvard, and certainly not such a small-minded one," replied Signe.

"You should be glad there's someone to teach you morals when you haven't any of your own."

"And lessons from a virgin to boot. You'll grow old waiting my thanks."

"I don't doubt it," said Edvard Ragnhilds-son.

Signe and Edvard recame Spring Green, but not in the best of spirits. Signe moved to Stephen's shop, but Edvard said to her, "You've made your bed, and it's not to my liking, so now I'll have to make my own."

Signe asked what he had in mind to do. Edvard said he meant to go west to Puget Sound, near the Far Ocean. There was a place there called the Order of the Sabbath Blessing. Edvard said they were well-known for their piety, even so far away as in Wisconsin. He thought they might look kindly upon him.

"I'm not sorry to stay," said Signe, "nor to see you go, since you feel as you do. But I can't think we'll get free each from the other as easily as that."

"No, likely not," said Edvard. He left Wisconsin for the west before the end of June.

Stephen in Kenosha

The Primate of the Church of the Second Rebirth at this time was called Jeremy Smithson. He was a small man with gray hair and the eyes of one who often laughed. He was now sixty-two winters old and looked likely to see several more years. Some call him the wisest of Wisconsin's Primates; others, the most crafty. But in any case, his enemies seldom laughed long. Jeremy had favored the bloodhands more often than not up to this time, and he had always sided with Stephen in disputes.

The first church courts met in April and tried the captives from Washington Island. They found all the four priests innocent and sent them out to parishes around the country. But they sent four of the five islanders to prison.

Stephen heard this result; he was unhappy that the courts had so lightly broken his promises to the islanders. He feared also that Jeremy might have turned from him; then one defeat might tide many more with it.

The Church Council called Stephen to Kenosha early in June to help in the midsummer celebrations, as they said. Most people in Spring Green took this as a mark of honor. Stephen decided to put the best face on his fears; he left home with a bodyguard of ten and festive clothes for all.

Jeremy called for Stephen on the afternoon of Midsummer's Eve. The Primate did not rise when Stephen came into the room. He said, "In some places they say you did just what you had to on Washington Island, and that no man could have done better. Perhaps that's so. Still, those priests you brought back tell it differently. They say you made captives of them and gave away many things they had already won from the islanders. It could be a hard thing for you; after all you did carry them off."

"Had I not, they'd be speaking from the grave, or not at all."

"No doubt. But they don't show much gratitude. They mean to press the charge against you as far as they can. Perhaps they'll even have luck. It won't help you that the case goes to the church court, where most of your witnesses can't speak."

"You talk in a friendly enough tone," said Stephen. "But I think you must have turned against me yourself, or such things wouldn't happen."

"You can think as you like. But many people beside the God-fearers fear you, and I have as many duties to them, and to the God-fearers, for that matter, as to you. What I hope is to delay the trial. With luck the suit could wait till you're out of danger; that's the more likely, since most of your enemies only want you out of the way for a time."

"I've stayed in Wisconsin because it seemed a home," said Stephen. "Now that it's turned on me, I'd just as soon leave it behind."

"For my part," said Jeremy, "I hope you'll stay. The church is bound to have a use for you soon. Still, you can go if you like. Just remember that flight's as much a sign of guilt here as elsewhere."

Stephen thought a time and said, "The only good in this is that you broke me when you broke my word to the islanders."

"Yes, and it may well be useful someday that people can still trust you."

"Useful to you." Stephen's voice was no longer steady as he spoke.

Jeremy came annoyed in his turn. "Useful to me. This church brings what little fairness there is in Wisconsin. I mean for it to live longer than I. Using your misfortune is the least of the things I'd do for her. And you—do you think all you did on Washington Island was kind and generous?"

Stephen looked at Jeremy a moment, then smiled all at once

and said, "It was a good piece of work, even so."

"So it was. Let the art be its own reward. Now to practical things. You must certainly leave the Green Hall. A possible kidnapper can't have a place of such trust. There's another cottage you can use instead. It's smaller than you're customed to, but near the village and with a garden. And I can tell my friends here that the townspeople are keeping an eye on you."

Stephen was no longer smiling. He said, "Your kindness has no bound. How long do you mean to hold on showing it?"

"So long as it suits me. Farewell; don't be rash."

Stephen recame Spring Green some days later. He left behind the bodyguard he had brought to Kenosha. But Jeremy sent ten men home with him to guard the way.

Stephen in Exile

Minna guessed that something was amiss when Stephen recame the hall, for she saw no one in his bodyguard she knew. She asked Stephen what this might tide. He told her how he had been treated and what the prospects were now. "But," said he, "no one will have much comfort from staying here. The yard they offer's not so bad. But it's overgrown, and the cottage hasn't been cleaned in years. I'd not count on much help to put things right, either."

Minna answered, "There's nothing fair in what's fallen you. Still, you ask a lot if you mean me to pay for your mistakes when you've ignored one warning after the next. I stand to lose honor if I leave you now, but you get no bad fame for leaving me the choice of that or living on with a cripple."

Stephen said, "I look for you to do just what profits you best."

"I won't disappoint you when you're so sure of me. But I don't think your pride has finished giving you trouble, even if your wife has."

Minna left Spring Green on the morning following and returned to her father's house in Ridgeway. Stephen moved to his new cottage, and the bodyguard went home to Kenosha. Stephen's marriage to Minna was soon annulled by the bishop's court in Beloit.

Stephen stayed alone in his cottage for most of the summer. He went out only for food and to borrow books from the abbot. Several people came to see him, for the most part soldiers who had fought at his side. He greeted them all civilly and said he was well when they asked after his health. But he would take no help, not even gifts from his guests' gardens. "I may not be highly placed," he said, "but I can live on my own when I must." And, in fact, he planted a garden for the summer and canned enough vegetables for the winter as well.

Nor would Stephen make any long reply when asked his plans. At the most he would say, "Wisconsin's my home; I'll not leave her willingly." People hardly knew how to take that; but they found Stephen so severe, especially toward himself, that they stopped coming to see him.

Signe also visited Stephen from time to time. She brought him presents of food and cloth which he did not refuse. Sometimes they played cards together for an hour or two. But they spoke little of Stephen's plight until one day when Signe said, "It's sad that you insist on being forsaken by every hand. Many people only wait for you to show a less forbidding face."

Stephen replied, "Friendship's a flower that dies at first frost, so they say. What sort of friend comes to laugh at a beaten man, in any case? I'll keep to myself, if it's all the same to you, or even if it isn't."

"That's up to you. But it's not the wise course."

"It is up to me, and you can leave me to myself as well, if you won't stop telling me what to do."

*　*　*

Signe went to Olivia and told her how the matter had fallen out. She finished by saying, "Your brother wants to hurt everyone he can just now, and that's not a surprise. But I'll do no more for him one way or another, though he is the dearest of men to me."

Olivia visited Stephen in her turn a week later. He greeted her and said, "I've not seen much of you since I found you that farm."

"I'm enough your sister to know when to leave you alone."

"There's no call to change your spots now."

"Perhaps not. But there is this, that you've insulted Signe who's my friend and might be more than that to you."

"I've put up with more than hurt feelings lately, so I'd not count her loss too highly."

"But she may, and she's the sort of woman who can be as difficult when she feels badly used as she's been kind to you this summer."

"If that's all you have to say, you needn't have come at all."

"There is another thing," said Olivia. "Many men have borne as great a loss as you, and no one grudges their being less than themselves for a time afterward. But only a fool holds on to his pain as you're doing and makes himself tiresome to everyone."

Stephen came angry at this and said, "I could as well listen to Signe as to you. At least she has a voice worth hearing." Olivia left and did not recome her brother's house for some time.

There was, however, one person with whom Stephen spoke more freely. This was the abbot who lived now in the Green Hall, and from whom Stephen borrowed books.

Once, it seemed to the abbot that Stephen was freer from care than usual. He asked Stephen about this, and the soldier replied, "To read a book helps. But also this, that I've learned it's better to serve the poor than the church."

"It's fortunate, then, that one serves the church by serving the poor."

"Sometimes that's true," said Stephen.

Douglas the Doctor

The story now tells of a man called Douglas, a short man with a limp, white-haired and long in the nose. He lived alone in the hills south from Spring Green.

Douglas had been a doctor before the war and well-liked. But when the bombs fell, he lost his family and soon after caught an illness that made his face red for some years. During this time, he traveled from one village to another, but often he had to continue on because people feared his face. He came to dress oddly and to call himself a witch; he thought in this way to scare villagers even more, until they came kind to him. But more frequently than not, they only drove him off the sooner.

At last Douglas came to Wisconsin and to the uplands. There he stayed easily enough; his neighbors were often odder than he. Douglas was no longer red in the face by this time, but he liked being a witch.

Douglas was known in Wisconsin for two things, first that he claimed to cure the sick and second that he caught snakes. His neighbors in the hills thought well of him on both counts, and he is still called the white witch there. But the villagers of Spring Green had their own doctors and few snakes. The stories there say that Douglas only cured those he had himself made sick, and that he could catch snakes because of a bargain he had with the devil. Even those who thought nothing of such tales thought badly of it that Douglas used the skeleton of a two-headed snake to guard his house from outsiders.

Douglas knew well enough what was said of him in Spring Green and seldom came there, especially after the shops refused to sell to him. But he decided to visit Signe even so when he heard that she had a new shop; he never found it easy to keep up stores on his own.

There was a full moon on the second Sunday in August. Douglas rode down to Signe's shop; he wore a gray cloak that hid him all but the nose. He arrived after dark and before midnight.

Signe heard someone at her door. She opened it, saw Douglas, and asked, "What help can you use, you who travel so late in the night?"

"I've come to buy some things from this shop."

"I see," said Signe. "Who are you?"

"My name is Douglas; some of my friends call me Saint Patrick, and here in town they think I'm a witch and no more than that. Take your choice. But if you've the wit to fear spells, you'll sell me what I need."

"On the contrary, I'd give you nothing if I feared magic. But as things stand, you're welcome and to take what you like."

Douglas came inside; he gathered together one thing and another until he had made a fair-sized pile on the table. These things he paid for, but others he could not find, in particular some of the spices he needed for his magic. He told Signe what he still missed and said, "I'd pay you well if you found those things for me."

"That's the sort of bargain I like," said Signe. Douglas agreed to come again in a month's time. He rode off to the south soon after midnight.

Signe's neighbors marked it that her lanterns burned late that night, and all Spring Green knew of Douglas's visit by morning. Some no longer shopped from Signe after that; others came all the more often from curiosity. They asked Signe of her visitor more than once, but she would say little of him. It seemed she would rather keep her thoughts to herself.

Douglas recame Spring Green after a month and with the full moon. He arrived just at midnight; Signe greeted him and said, "Be welcome and have some wine."

The wine in Wisconsin at that time was very sweet and made from cherries that grow in the counties near Death's Door. Douglas and Signe drank together. Douglas said, "I'm a happy man to have found an honest shopkeeper after so many years." And, when he finished the wine, "Let's see what you've found for me."

But Signe stayed at the table and said, "By all means. But it's only right if you say how you mean to pay for it all first."

"You needn't worry on that count." Douglas took a sack from his cloak and poured from it silver coins, a gold watch, and a knife made of bronze. He said, "You can take what you think fair out of all this."

Signe looked at the pile of metal and said, "This is far more than a fair price, as well you know. Still, I've heard that 'gold gotten by moonlight glitters no good,' and I doubt that silver and bronze are much better."

"It's a long time since anyone thought to teach me curses," said Douglas. "And I think you took my coins a month ago, too."

"Yes. But one needn't repeat mistakes."

"Perhaps not. What price have you in mind if you don't like my money? I looked for better from you than that I should ride off empty-handed."

Signe looked at the table once more. "It's said you cure the sick."

"Sometimes I do."

"And that you know a good deal of snakes?"

"That's possible."

"Then here's my price," said Signe, "that you teach me what you know of those things."

Douglas's face showed no expression.

Signe went on, "I see you think the price steep. But I'll bring you whatever more you need and for so long as the lessons last."

Douglas now spoke and said, "You can't think to do this. No one's dared my door in years, and that's no surprise when it's guarded by the devil's own double serpent." He took up his money from the table and went to the door.

"The devil would find a new disguise," said Signe. But Douglas went through the door as she spoke.

• • •

Three nights later Douglas recame Signe's shop. She greeted him well; he said, "Have you thought on what the gossips say, that I'm so mad a man I scare even faithless folk? They don't often lie."

"I've heard that," said Signe, "but many can be thought mad for their own reasons."

Douglas went quiet for a minute's time, then said, "I'll take your bargain, if still you offer it."

"Done," said Signe. She brought out all the things she had saved for Douglas and gave him a round of cheese for good measure. Signe and Douglas shook hands to seal the bargain, and he rode off once more.

The villagers of Spring Green soon decided where Signe must go when she left her shop behind in the months following. Whenever she went off, some of them thought never to see her again. But just as frequently, she recame the village, and no evil could be seen at her door. One opinion had it that worse must fall her later if she came free of harm now.

In all this time, Signe hardly spoke with Stephen, even when they chanced to meet on the street. But it was said she still thought more of him than of any other. As for Stephen, his eyes were never far from Signe on feast days. But Olivia said, "I don't think those two will ever see eye to eye for long."

Farmers Come to Stephen

Time now passes to the third summer of Stephen's disgrace. There was a far better harvest than usual in Wisconsin that year. Many growers looked to have enough for themselves and a good deal more beside, even the smallest among them. But the prices dropped all through the year; they were so low by the end of summer and into harvesttime that there was little gain in it to bring crops to

market. Many thought, in fact, that the market only ate away all
the good the weather had brought.

Some of the farmers made their way to Kenosha to ask help
from the church. They said they had always given the fathers
what they asked in the past, and that this was the time to be
repaid.

But the church answered by sending out a single priest to talk
with the farmers. This priest was a gray-haired man with one
slack eye and the manner of an ice floe. He had never been made
a bishop because he was too widely feared. Now he told the
farmers, "Nowhere is the easy life to be found; and this problem
of yours is your own fault, in any case, since you've tried to sell
too much at once. For that matter, the church is as badly placed
as you are, since we get so little for the tithes you send us in
kind."

The farmers grumbled rather more than less after this speech,
though it was true enough that most of them had been willing to
share their glut with the church. But some said it was better to
blame the Argentines than even the coldest of their own men.
Some said too that the Primate Jeremy would have been more
generous, if left to himself.

A group of small-holders came to Stephen's house from the
valley east and west from Spring Green. It was then early in
September; the price of wheat had fallen to a fifth of its customed
level. The farmers chose a man called Walter to speak for them,
a slightly built man with thin, gray eyes and the reputation of
being the third-best lawyer in Wisconsin; Walter was also counted
a difficult man in a fight. He said, "We have heard, friend Stephen, that your luck has lately been less than it was. Yet we
remember too that you never lacked courage in the past. We hope
you will help us who are members of the church, even when
there's nothing you can do for the fathers in Kenosha."

"I'd help you and gladly," said Stephen, "if I could. But what do you suggest? It's a good bet that my voice would poison any plea just now."

"You know more of that than we," said Walter, "but we might help each other in some different way."

Stephen looked at the steadsmen and said, "I hadn't looked to fight again so soon. There's no point to thinking about it now, either, unless I have men behind me who are willing to die, if need be."

The farmers talked all at once. After a time, Walter spoke once more; the farmers went quiet for him. "I can promise you fifteen men from among us who are here."

Stephen replied, "Fifteen will be enough to do something useful." He told his visitors to go home and wait further word.

Nothing happened for some days after that. But Stephen seemed more preoccupied than usual.

Rumors

The Argentines usually bought a good deal of grain from Wisconsin in the summer, made it into alcohol, and shipped it from a port they had at Green Bay. They bought enough in good years that it could not all be sent at once, but some must wait for later ships. The Argentines built many silos to store what had to be held; four of them were larger than any others in Wisconsin. All the granaries were now as full as they were like to get.

The Argentines had also cut back the wages they paid to the men who worked the docks because, as they said, the price of food no longer required the higher pay of other years. More than a few of the townspeople came unhappy over this, but the Argentines sent a shipload of soldiers to Green Bay. There seemed nothing for the townspeople to do about the matter after that.

• • •

Stephen called for the men Walter had promised early in October. They left Spring Green in company and were away for about ten days.

Two days after Stephen returned from his travels, there came news from Green Bay to Spring Green. It was said that in the middle of one night, some bombs had set fire to one of the main granaries. Then the townspeople, and especially those who had lost wages working on the docks, came out into the street and fought with the firemen. The Argentines soon called for their soldiers to push back the townspeople. Bombs then burst in a second silo, and soon after in the other two as well. These blasts unnerved the Argentines, and they fell back to their camp south from the town and a bit west from the River of Foxes.

A bit later still, an oil tank near the river caught fire, and the crowd had no trouble to drive the firemen away. They went through the streets after that and took or broke whatever they wished; in the morning, eight people were dead from the town, and a soldier as well. All the main granaries were burned past repair, along with many houses.

The Argentines came annoyed at this turn of events and sent more soldiers, so to discourage the town from being unruly any further. In the end, though, they did buy grain to replace what had been lost. The price stayed much the same, but many farmers were able to sell what they had been ready to burn, especially the freeholders and tenants whom the church favored for the new sales. But the townspeople of Green Bay fared less well.

There were rumors that Stephen must have had a part in the riots at Green Bay. Stephen answered all the gossip by saying, "The Argentines deserve the credit for making so many soldiers and so willing." This did not quiet everyone who heard it, however, and sometimes Stephen also said, "It sounds too sloppy a fight for any captain to want."

For all that Stephen said, there were still those who came from long distances to see him, even through the heaviest snows, then as well. Sometimes they asked his help about one thing or another, or else they only wanted to see him. He told his visitors that he would like to do more for them, but that he could not, when the church had tied his hands so closely.

Stephen and Signe Marry

Soon after the riot in Green Bay, Stephen came to Signe's house. He said, "I don't know how it is I've forgotten you so far and for so long. Perhaps you can forgive me for it now, though, since I'm no longer so gloomy."

Signe asked Stephen inside then, and also several times afterward. At last, early in December, Stephen asked Signe to marry him.

Signe said nothing for a time, and then, "I'd like that also. But first I'll have to be clear about what we're getting into, since marriages don't always last."

"Your first answer pleases me better than the second," said Stephen. "Perhaps you should say just what you mean."

"This, that the money I have now is what I've made from my own work. I want to be sure of keeping it, however things turn out between the two of us."

"I don't see how you can speak so coldly of the heart's love," said Stephen.

"Then you don't know me very well—or yourself, for that matter."

Stephen said, "At the least, I know you aren't the most straightforward of women. What you ask now isn't the normal way of things, but I won't let it hold us back. On the other hand, since we've come to asking favors one from the other, I have one to ask of you."

"Yes?" said Signe.

"You've spent a good deal of time with this man Douglas. I'd like that to stop. It won't sit well with people here if I have a wife who talks with witches. My fortunes rest a good deal on how they think of me."

"You ask a bit more of me than I do of you. Still, I'll stop from seeing Douglas once we're married and for so long as you deal well with me."

Stephen thought about these words for a minute and said, "One could think you as much a lawyer as a doctor."

Signe laughed at that, and soon Stephen laughed as well.

Signe traveled up to Douglas's house in the uplands twice more. At last she told him of her agreement with Stephen and said, "It seems I can't have everything just as I'd like."

Douglas replied, "You forced yourself on me in the first place; now you leave on a whim. It's a small enough loss." But a few minutes later he spoke again, and more softly, "You've been a better student than I feared, and your stores a great help. May you have a long life and happy. One thing more you might do for me, and that's to make sure people keep on fearing my house as much as they used to."

Signe agreed to do what she could and gave him a bundle of things from her shop. She said, "I'll send you more if I can."

Signe fell from her horse on the way home and cut her cheek. Her neighbors asked her what had happened, but Signe would say nothing. She did take to carrying a cross wherever she went after dark, though.

The most common story told of Signe after this was that she had had a duel of magic with Douglas and had come near a bad end. Some claimed to see the spirits loosed in that battle flying around Signe's head still, and some also said she deserved her fate.

The new year came soon after. Signe drew up some papers to say that all she then owned was hers forever. Stephen signed his oath to these papers, and Signe put them out of the way.

Stephen and Signe married each other early in February, on a day both cold and gentle with snow. They lived together in Stephen's cottage after that, but Signe continued to work in her shop. No more is told of them until the spring, except that Signe came pregnant.

Stephen Regains Favor

In the days after the Green Bay riots, Jeremy Smithson, Primate of Wisconsin, decreed that the greater part of new grain sales must go to small-holders and not to the landlords or to the church. This measure displeased many God-fearers both inside the church and out.

The winter following did little to reassure them. Jeremy sent two of their highest men out to the countryside in December. Worse still were the laws he spoke at the new year. The first of these let a tenant appeal to the church fathers when a landlord imposed a fine without leave. Up to that time, a tenant could only go to a bishop's court, and few bishops would rule against any but the smallest of landlords. The second law said that no tenant could be forced to move from a piece of land he had worked five years or longer.

Some landlords took these laws well enough, either because they had feared worse, or because they hoped to see Jeremy's hand strengthened against the Argentines. But most of the God-fearers were unrestful. They met together all through the winter, and openly. Nothing came of their talks at this time or, as it happened, for some time after. But Jeremy was a prudent man; he began to rally what forces he could to his side.

It was the custom of spring for the Primate of Wisconsin to travel around the church's domains to hear how people spoke of the world after the winter. Jeremy went south in the year following the Green Bay riots, to the lower Wisconsin River valley, among other places. He did not fail to visit Stephen in Spring Green.

Stephen and Signe welcomed Jeremy with food and drink.

Stephen and the Primate then sat to talk one with the other in a small room to the back of Stephen's cottage. They had spoken only a short time, however, when they heard the sound of a crowd of people from outside. Stephen said, "It must be farmers from down the valley who want to see you."

Jeremy replied, "Perhaps they come more for you than for me."

"They can see me anytime."

The noise now came so loud that Stephen and Jeremy could no longer talk easily. The two men went through the house to the front door. Jeremy stepped through first. There were nearly a thousand men and women gathered in the street outside. They went still when they saw Jeremy.

Stephen stepped out a few seconds later. The gathering made more noise even than before, so that no single voice could be heard.

When the throng was once more still, Jeremy thanked them for coming and said he knew better than to try to send them away before his meeting with Stephen was finished. "But," said he, "you must remember to let us hear one another."

Stephen said nothing, but only waved his hand.

Stephen and Jeremy came inside together, and to their back room. Signe had left flowers in the window while they were gone. Jeremy spoke first: "I see you're the master of a fair-sized flock." He gave Stephen the cross that showed he was once again a captain.

"They're all loyal followers of the church," said Stephen.

Jeremy said nothing to that, but offered Stephen the Green Hall he had held before. Stephen said, "I'd rather let the abbot hold his place there. I remember as well how the church backed me before; perhaps my neighbors here won't be so cautious."

"That's as you wish," said Jeremy, "though I'd think it safer if your comfort depended more on the church."

• • •

The two men went back outside and stood on the porch that overlooked the street. This porch was wooden, painted white, with a white railing at the front and a fir tree on either side. Signe joined the two men; the three of them stood, dark-clad, under a cold and brilliant sun, to face the crowd. Jeremy spoke first and said that Stephen was once more a captain, but that he had chosen to live among his many friends in the village. The crowd of people cheered their Primate for some minutes. Stephen also spoke, and only for a short time. He said that everyone should trust in the church; it always found a way to heal whatever wounds a man might have. The crowd cheered once more and for a longer time than Stephen had spoken. At the last, they carried Jeremy all the way to the Green Hall, where he meant to stay the night.

Stephen was more than a little proud of himself after this. But Signe said he would do better to think of more than his own fate.

The Birth of Michael Signes-son

It seemed that a storm might break this year in the quarrel between Jeremy and the God-fearers. But prices came higher than in the year before; the northmen were still unhappy, but landlords from the west refused to move against the church. Then others, from the south, refused as well. In the end, peace came to Wisconsin, after all.

Signe gave birth to a son shortly after the new year. He was in all ways a fair child, save that his left foot had no toes and seemed misshapen.

But Stephen was glad in his son; he said, "I've seen many victories that cost more than a foot." And Signe was even fonder of the boy. She insisted to name him Michael after her own father. Olivia came to be Michael's godmother.

The custom in Wisconsin in those days was to think a mis-formed child an unwanted child, or even an unlucky one. Some the villagers who mistrusted Signe said that she must secretly hate her son; the more common opinion was that God Himself had turned against her for her unnatural ways, especially in talking with Douglas. More than one came to Stephen and told him he must turn his back on so unhappy a wife and child.

Stephen would not listen to such talk at first. But in time he came to hear it not only from the faint of heart, but also from those he most trusted to stand with him in case of trouble. After some months, a miller called Jed Gould came more bold than the others and began to call Signe the mother of monsters. Stephen complained, but not very loudly. It was also marked that he had fewer smiles for his son than he had had at the beginning, at least in public. But when Signe asked Stephen what these things might tide, he said only that he had many things on his mind.

Signe came annoyed in the end at the way matters stood with Stephen. She complained that he had turned his back on her at the first sign of trouble, whatever he liked to say. Stephen said, "I'm as kind to you at home as ever, and to Michael as well. But I can't forget other people who need me just to please you; it's not my doing that they distrust you so far."

Signe then said, "Your private heart will soon be as hard as your public one, if it isn't already."

Not long after, Signe sent word to Douglas that he could come to Spring Green to buy whatever he needed. Douglas came late in the summer, at the full moon as before. He left flowers for Signe as a sign of his visit.

This journey of Douglas's angered Stephen. He said to Signe, "Many a promise I made to you when we married, and every one of them kept. Now you think nothing of breaking the only word you gave me."

"I promised not to see Douglas as long as you treated well

with me, and that's just what I've done. Now that I see how little you think of me and of Michael as well, I mean to do just what I think right."

Stephen replied, "I've suffered insult and worse for Michael, and willingly; he's my son. But you—you're hurting everything I hope to do, and care nothing about it." At last he said, "At any rate, it will go badly for you if you meet that man again."

"Take your threats somewhere else; perhaps others will believe them."

As it happened, however, Douglas stayed from Spring Green for many months after that.

Ragnhild's Family in Norway

Now it must be told what happened with Ragnhild when first she came back to Norway, and to the farm that had been her father's.

Ragnhild was one of three daughters of a man called Arne Eiriksen and his wife, Ashild. Ashild died during the war, but Arne continued to live on his farm at Eidfjord, along with Ragnhild's sisters, Ingeborg and Inger. Arne's farm was a fairly large one for the Fjordlands, with a stream to cut it in half. But Arne was only an indifferent farmer.

No one in Norway thought to see Ragnhild again, and it seemed that Ingeborg and Inger were to inherit all the farm after Arne. But Ragnhild had been Arne's favorite daughter, and he was not willing to leave her out of the account. He divided the farm into three parts, with each daughter to have one. But Ingeborg and Inger would share Ragnhild's part if she never claimed it. Arne died soon after deciding things in this manner, in the third winter after bombsfall.

The two sisters, Ingeborg and Inger, now went in different ways. Inger never married, but grew troubled at the many fights

THE FAMILY OF ARNE OF EIDFJORD

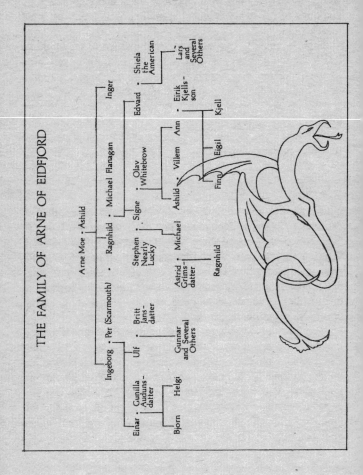

of those days over land and other possessions. She also came lonely because most her friends had died in the war, and she would make no new ones for fear that they might die as well. After a few years she decided to stay in Eidfjord no longer, but to live instead in an old mountain *saeter,* which had always been her parents' but which had been left empty in recent years. She told Ingeborg, "That's a lonely spot, and more to my liking than this."

As for Inger's share of Arnes-stead, she left it to Ingeborg and her husband Per to use as they pleased. "But," said she, "I can't think Father meant to leave Ragnhild out of any division." She let Ingeborg to have only half the share outright, but the rest must be held for Ragnhild. In this way, all of Arnes-stead passed into the hands of Per and Ingeborg, though they could claim only half of it for themselves.

Ingeborg was already married to Per when the war came. It seemed for a time that she must be a widow, for Per was caught near Oslo in the worst of times. But he was a clever man and meant to see more hardship; he lived on even when most in the East did not. Per was called Scarmouth ever after, however, from a wound he picked up during his wandering back to the Westland. He was a good-enough-looking man otherwise, and valuable to people in Hardanger when he helped fight against the wandering bands who passed through in the first years.

Ingeborg built many new things on her land and fixed old ones, so that the farm came a more important place than it had been under Arne. She was also willing to help her neighbors in many things, and gained the reputation of being the third most open-handed woman in Hardanger.

Per and Ingeborg had two children who lived past childhood, sons called Ulf and Einar. Einar was the elder by two years, a

born farmer who spent most his childhood helping Ingeborg fix
the stead. He was a handsome lad and a bit stout, not the sort to
waste time on dreams. Ulf was slight, darker than his brother,
and a quiet child.

For many years Ingeborg and her family used Arnes-stead as
they liked. They followed the lead of several others and let tenants
to live on the land with them to help with the crops and to take
their side in disputes. But no one thought to claim any part of
their land.

Ingeborg came to look for the time when Ulf and Einar would
take over the whole of the land in their turn; it seemed likely that
Einar would have his way with most of it, since Ulf was more
at home on a boat than a farm.

Ingeborg took sick with a wasting cough in the year that Einar
was seventeen. This was also the year that many calves died in
Hardanger. Ingeborg died early in the following spring, leaving
behind on Arnes-stead only Per Scarmouth of all those who had
known life before death.

Per was a strong man still and got on with his life better than
most. Even so, he was coming wrinkled, and his scar showed a
cruel white; he left many parts the farm for his sons to handle.
Many people thought he would soon pass the land itself on to
Ulf and Einar. This seemed most likely in the year when Einar
was twenty winters old and had just married Gunilla, the daughter
of Strongman Audun. Einar and Gunilla made a fine pair, both
tall and fair, known for working hard and keeping up appearance.
They stayed on land that Gunilla had from her father in Kvanndal,
but people said that the stead at Eidfjord would suit them better;
it was larger and flatter.

Ragnhild Returns

Ragnhild Arnes-datter came to Hardanger late in the summer of
this year, the same in which she left Africa. Most of Eidfjord
welcomed her; her family had always been well-regarded before.

Ragnhild moved out to a small house on her part of the farm. Per welcomed her, and so did Inger when she heard the news. But Per's son Einar was not so well pleased.

Einar's words counted for little with Ragnhild, however. By the end of the fall, she had made her house a lasting place to live. The rooms in Ragnhild's house were unlike any others in Norway; she kept in them masks and wood carvings from Africa. Per liked these things so well that he came to spend more time at Ragnhild's house than at his own. About this time also, he started to take a greater interest in the work of the whole farm.

Per went to see his son Einar in the following spring and said, "Ragnhild and I mean to live together as husband and wife from now on. But I don't think we need all the farm for ourselves; we're giving half to you and Ulf to do with as you like. Perhaps Ulf will let you use his share until he has a mind to reclaim it."

Einar thought little of this speech. It seemed him that Ragnhild had stolen half the land that should have been his, and his father to boot. He said, "I see you think this a generous offer you've made. But it seems something of an insult to me, considering how much more I've done for the place than Aunt Ragnhild has. Beside, as things stand, it's bound to be more a burden than a help; it's smaller than we need for our place in things here, and far from Gunilla's place as well."

Per called this an ungrateful answer, not least because "there was no need to give you anything."

But Einar said, "If things were as they should be, you'd care more for my mother's wishes, and you'd not prefer that woman over your own sons."

Per left Kvanndal that same day. Einar asked Gunilla what they might do with their new land. She answered, "You're right that we shouldn't move there, if only because of the people we'd live beside. It seems a shame to let the whole thing go to waste, though. Here's what I think you should do: go out there and put a dam across the stream so the water backs up. Then we'll have a place to swim in summer, and perhaps some fish to go with. But you should choose the spot well, so the water can back onto precious Ragnhild's land. Then we can show her something of the way we think about her."

Einar thought this a fine idea and saw to it as soon as he could.

Ragnhild was not slow to notice that Einar's lake was in among her potatoes; and it made her no more prone to like her stepson. She went to Per and said, "Now I see that this nephew of mine is meaner than five bottles of cat piss. I doubt that we need to see him again for some time. But meanwhile, we must do something about this pond of his."

Per said that Ragnhild had the right of the matter, but that it might not be easy to force the issue when the dam was built in a place where the stream was on Einar's side the land. "It won't do for me to cross over and knock the thing down," said he, "since it's a bad thing when a father and son fight."

Ragnhild replied, "I didn't think to see you brought low quite so easily."

Per was silent a moment and then said, "I have heard that Mistress Gunilla has a great dislike for these sunflowers that grow new since the war. We could plant some on our side the pond, and she might get even less pleasure from the thing than we do."

Ragnhild said, "That's more the sort of thing I thought to hear from you in the first place."

The following year, Ragnhild plowed up all the potatoes that edged the lake and planted sunflowers in their place. These soon grew to a great height and spread themselves to the wind.

Einar and Gunilla came to see their land early in the summer; they were not so well pleased as they had hoped to be. Einar asked his father what might be the meaning of ruining their lake.

Per said that it was the custom in Africa to eat flower seeds, and also, "We thought they would go nicely with Ragnhild's hair when she's out working."

"Nothing will help hair as gray as hers," said Einar. But he and Gunilla stayed for only two days, and otherwise let their tenants to work the land.

Olav Whitebrow

Einar's younger brother, Ulf Pers-son, went to sea every year, at first to fish and later for trade. For several years he sailed with a man called Olav. This Olav had grown in the south on a small farm with his older brother Sverre and his mother Astrid. They were a poor family, and their land stony. Olav's father foretold the weather in the times before the war. Some say that he worshipped the old god Thor, and in any case that he was killed by Christians who disagreed with him during the first dark times.

When Olav was fourteen winters old, he went with a neighbor called Oddvar Kinnbein into the mountains. Oddvar was older than Olav and stronger. The two of them came on a house from the old times that had stood untended many years. They found many things inside and put the best of them into two sacks to carry home. One thing they found was a silver belt buckle with clear gems on it, set into the pattern of the constellation Orion. Olav very much wanted this as his own; Oddvar thought it should be his. They quarreled over the matter all the way home.

When they reached Olav's house, Oddvar thought to take the buckle by force. But Sverre heard the argument and came outside. He said to Oddvar, "I'm the better match, if you want to fight."

Oddvar replied, "It's still nothing to fear."

Sverre and Oddvar fought with swords until Oddvar was badly hurt and Sverre dead. Oddvar took the buckle and went home; but he too died within a few days.

. . .

Olav now gave his mother an oath that he would never bear arms in a quarrel, however great the provocation. This is told as the reason that Olav never fought in after times, though he was skilled with several weapons, especially the throwing knife. But others say that he never liked the danger of fighting, in any case.

However that is, Olav began to travel and to learn of many things, particularly of fish and of the law in the various parts of Norway. He was first able to plead at the Southland Thing in his nineteenth year, and he came a skilled net-mender. It was said of him that he could do anything except play music. But he was also a silent and untrusting man in those days; some say he took his brother's death to heart. Olav was then tall and quite thin, with black hair and brows and a sharp chin, which he kept always shaven.

After some years, Olav married a woman called Gudrun; she soon bore him a daughter. But these two died both of disease in Olav's twenty-eighth year, while he was yet at sea. This was the year that Ragnhild grew her sunflowers for Einar.

When Olav heard of Gudrun's death, he thought that all who were close to him were bound to die. He did not stay in the Southland longer, but came away with Ulf and on to Hardanger. But his hair turned white on the way and left only the brows black. It was in this way that Olav gained the name Whitebrow.

Olav hoped to break his bad luck by sailing oversea further than Europe in the year following. Ships in those days often started from Norway in the spring to trade Arctic goods south in Europe. Afterwards, the ships usually recame home, but they sometimes crossed the ocean to deal in the Caribbean and up the coast of America. The longer trips were dangerous for that the only goods carried from the Caribbean were smugglers'; nonetheless, they paid well to those with daring.

Ulf also thought to trade in America. He and Olav agreed to take a boat together, and to let Olav stay behind in America after the heavy work was done. "It may comfort me to see new places," said he, "and I can hope to find something that will profit us later on as well."

Ragnhild heard of this plan late in the winter. She called on Olav and said, "I don't know that you'll like to help me, but if so it might be a help to you as well. My two children went on to America when I came here. They were bound for a place called Wisconsin, but they've sent me no word how things are for them. Up to now, there's been no way for me to send a thing to them, either. But if you go that way, you might be able to take them my greeting."

"Wisconsin's as good a goal as any," said Olav, "but I promise nothing certain."

Ragnhild was content with these words. She gave Olav a box of dominoes and a music box with a bear that danced on its top. She said, "My daughter Signe first played with this bear when she was small; and Edvard, her brother, made me a present of these dominoes while yet we lived in Africa." She also gave him letters for her children and said, "They won't have forgotten what you give them from me, so they should care for you as they are able."

Olav took all the things he was given and promised to take them to the right places, if he could.

Ulf's ship took its trip well; neither honor nor fortune went wanting for captain or crew on all the voyage to America. Olav parted from the company there, and the others recame Norway before the winter and without incident. This was in the year Michael Signes-son was born.

Nothing is told of Olav's trip by foot through America up to the time he came to Wisconsin late in October. He had no trouble there to hear of Signe and her famous husband, and soon came to Spring Green.

Olav gave Signe her mother's greeting along with the music

box and the letter. When Signe saw the dancing bear she said, "This is a most welcome thing you've brought." She read the letter and made ready a room for Olav to stay in. Then she said, "The winter is nearly on us; I trust you'll make this place yours until the spring."

Olav replied, "It's easy to see that Ragnhild Arnes-datter makes no mistake of her children and their kindness." He agreed to stay. But it seemed that there was a coolness between Stephen and Olav.

Two Farmers Oppose Jeremy

During the summer before Olav came, the God-fearers once again met together. They came near to agreeing to oppose Jeremy, but those from the west still feared a confrontation and refused to go along. Then the others mostly agreed to wait another year before acting.

The two largest landowners from the north were not content with this delay, however, and met several times more in private. They were Jack O'Brien and Joseph Dougherty; their lands lay next each other, near Rhinelander, and where the birch forests begin.

The time for sending tithes to church came not long after. But Jack and Joseph sent neither cash nor crop to Kenosha. The church fathers at first took no note of this, but pretended that there was some mistake that would soon come right. But they knew other landlords would be watchful, and that many would follow the lead if they thought it a safe thing to do.

After two weeks with no word from Jack and Joseph, Jeremy sent a pair of messengers to mind them of their duties and also to say that the Council was little customed to showing mercy to its enemies.

The two messengers came first to Jack's house. He told them, "The church hasn't helped me for a long time; they've no reason to look for me to pay them." The messengers said nothing in reply to that because of the many men facing them.

They went on instead and came to Joseph's house, some way off to the west. Joseph asked them if they had been to see his friend O'Brien; the messengers said that they had. He asked them what Jack had said, and they told him that as well. "In that case," said Joseph, "his answer is mine as well."

But one of the messengers was bolder than the other; he said, "We can't change your mind; but this we can tell you, that the church will take all your land and do what they like with it if you continue to keep your tithes to yourselves."

Joseph was a strong man and not the sort to bear insult lightly. He told two of his men to grab the man who spoke and hold his head down. Joseph took an ax from the wall and cut off the messenger's head. He said to the remaining man, "I've often heard that 'two heads are better than one,' and I wonder if it's true. Take this one to friend Jeremy. Tell him it's my guess that he'll need more than a pair of wits to put paid to us."

The second messenger returned with his friend's head to Kenosha and spoke to Jeremy as he had been told. Jeremy listened and said, "They also say that the bearer of bad news bears the blame. But in this case, your friend's paid a high price for both of you."

Jeremy now called the Church Council to him and explained how things stood. He said, "We dare not to ignore these men or treat them lightly." He asked leave to send an army to crush the landlords.

All the Council agreed that Joseph's act was a threat to the church and an outrage. But some thought it understandable, considering how well the bloodhands had fared lately. They favored sending a delegation to Rhinelander to discuss the matter further.

But Jeremy said, "These two have cut themselves off from

God and His church just as they cut our man's head off. If you treat with them more, I can no longer be Primate here; everyone knows where I have stood; they'll have no reason to trust me longer."

The Council agreed to let Jeremy have his way. The Primate sent word to Stephen that same afternoon to tell him what had passed. Jeremy asked Stephen to solve the problem in any way he thought fit and promised the full backing of the church. Jeremy also wrote that secrecy was rare in Kenosha; the Rhinelanders were like to know what they faced.

Stephen had thought he might have work to do in this year; he had already chosen his lieutenants and arranged stores in case something came up. He had little trouble to organize a large force to press the attack against Jack and Joseph in the north when Jeremy's letter arrived.

But Stephen made no move to march against the northerners for two months, or until the middle of December, when he judged that Jack and Joseph would no longer expect to see him. He used the time instead to prepare what he needed for a winter campaign.

When Stephen's force did march, they moved so quickly that they surprised Jack's farm before the people there had taken up their defenses, and so won an easy victory.

The fight for Joseph's farm was not so easy, however. There the defenders were ready and held a group of houses that could not be approached save across open fields that sloped down from ridges north and south. Stephen besieged Joseph for three days. Then, on a cloudless night and before the moon rose, he sent half his soldiers down the hill south from the farm; these soldiers were dressed all in white and mounted on white skis. They succeeded in coming near the buildings. When the moon rose soon after midnight, the rest of Stephen's men started down the hill also and drew the fire of the defenders. This gave the first troops time to storm the buildings and so defeat Joseph's men.

• • •

After the battle, Stephen took those who still lived of Jack's family and Joseph's to Rhinelander town and put them all to death. But he let the tenants who had fought against him to go free, and allowed them to divide the two estates among themselves.

Many in Wisconsin were scared when they heard what sort of mercy Stephen had shown. But others thought it as well that the church fathers in Kenosha would get no chance to undo the good Stephen had done.

Signe, Olav, and Douglas

Signe and Olav stayed in Spring Green while Stephen was away in the north. Olav was a quiet guest and spent many of his days embroidering cloth. He seemed to come more cheerful as time passed, however.

One day, Olav was near to finishing a peacock. Signe asked him, "What is this work you spend so much time on?"

"It's mostly a thing I've learned to do while I'm alone and far from my fishnets."

"It's good work that you do, even so."

"Yes," said Olav, "the hands are clever when they have the chance."

The evening following, Olav gave Signe the peacock he had made. Signe thanked him and said, "I could wish you had come to America sooner, you who are so gentle a man."

Olav said, "Not everybody in Norway thought me either gentle or lucky. Many of them have died after knowing me too well."

"Then you must think that you live now in a different world; perhaps it will be luckier for your friends."

"Perhaps," Olav said. But in the end, he stayed that night with

Signe and afterward until Stephen's return. Signe looked on him with even greater favor after that.

Olav made ready to leave early in the spring. He spoke a last time with Signe and said, "I have heard that in the old days a woman would give herself to wait three years for her lover. I give you this promise, that my life is yours if you claim it in Norway before the end of three years. But if not, I'll count myself free to do as I like."

"No one should wait for me, Olav; I do not ask it of you."

"Nonetheless, I mean to do as I say."

Olav left Wisconsin then and left Ragnhild's present for Edvard behind. He recame Norway late in October of the same year.

Douglas, Signe's friend from the uplands, also came to Spring Green with the spring. He dragged a cart of books behind him and came to Stephen's door one evening.

Stephen saw him and said, "It's bad enough to have one of Signe's men all the winter without another at the door." He went out to meet Douglas and asked, "What brings you here?"

"I've heard only good things of your work in the north," replied Douglas. "Still, it's Signe I've come to see."

"I've given my word she'll never see you here."

"Then you'll have to break your word. Or else, I'll make your house sink into the ground."

"That's a stupid threat," said Stephen.

Douglas took a bottle from his cloak and threw it onto the porch behind Stephen. It broke and began to smoke. Stephen stepped back to the spot and found that his foot went through the floor. He said, "It's Signe you want; you're welcome to her."

Signe now came outside to see Douglas. She saw that his cloak was as long as always but a bit greasy with age, that he kept his right hand at his side, and that what showed of his face was thin. Douglas said, "I've found some charms you left in my books. It wasn't very kind of you to plant them there."

"I've done nothing of the sort," said Signe.

"Don't teach me my business; I can recognize a charm as well as you can. Take these books you've poisoned. Much good may they do you." He threw the books onto the porch with his left hand, overturned the cart, and left without speaking more.

Signe took the books inside. Stephen told her to burn them; he then left for the night. The books were of medicine and other arts; Signe hid them well and burned some others, so to have ashes to show for her work.

Two weeks later, some upland farmers saw a flame burn up from Douglas's house. A black cloud of smoke followed soon after. Some of them went to see the place and could find nothing of man nor house, save for the stone cellar and some charred wood.

Some way off, however, they did find a tree with a paper nailed to it. This note said, "I go to fight the demons of the night. If my craft fail me, I leave nothing in this world, save my double-headed serpent. That can go to anyone who finds it, and its power and curses with it."

But no one could find the skeleton itself, though more than a few tried. Most people thought Douglas had found a way to hide it in the books he left for Signe. Signe said nothing of the matter, however, and no one saw her with the skeleton, however closely she was watched.

Jeremy Makes an Offer to Stephen

Stephen had word to join Jeremy on his spring tour. He was delayed because of his doubts about both Olav and Douglas, but in the end came to join the Primate's party in Beloit.

Jeremy stopped watching a parade to talk with Stephen. The Primate said, "I hoped to see you sooner than this; perhaps your work is the sort that needs rest."

"Even the bravest soldier quails when he has a wife to fight."

"So I've heard. Now, tell me how you think I can best use your victory at Rhinelander."

"You could do nothing, if you like," said Stephen. "The God-fearers should be fearful and even less at one than they were."

"You think that's the best idea?"

"No. You'll do better to break them here—especially if you mean to live many more years. They won't always be so scared. And they have better reason to hate you now than before."

"We agree about many things," said Jeremy. "And if something's to be done, you're the man to do it. As to long life, it's best to be ready, whatever happens.

"I fear there's not much I can do to help you; my hands aren't all my own, as you know. Still, you can be sure nothing will be done to stop you, should you find an army to lead against them; I can decree that you go on the church's business, if you succeed."

"Armies are expensive," said Stephen.

"So they are. But by law, you keep four parts in five of the plunder when you go on the church's errand at your own expense."

Stephen said, "An army may be hard to find, even so. But it's good work to fight for the church and fairness and treasure all at once."

"Yes," said Jeremy. "A little blood now may help matters later on. Still, you'll do well to remember two things: you're meant to chasten the God-fearers, not to destroy them; and you are a captain, not a king."

Signe Flees Wisconsin

Stephen wrote: "This offer of Jeremy's was a remarkable chance for any captain, nothing less than a license to work a revolution in Wisconsin, if I could. But the obstacles were no less formidable than the opportunity. The God-fearers could field an army much larger than I had any hope to command, provided only that they could unite. They also had the wealth to bury any foe, given time.

"I, on the other hand, could count on the discipline of people who had been with me before, and on the resentment of peasants in many parts of Wisconsin. The best hope was to use the small farmers' hatred to start a number of small rebellions, so to keep most the landlords occupied at home. Then a fairly small main force might defeat the God-fearers one by one."

Stephen met with about thirty men from previous campaigns, those whom he trusted most. They planned together how to get the peasants to rise in good order and at the right time, and how to raise and arm the main force.

All Stephen's plans required money, however. Quite a few of his friends were willing to help, and Stephen himself sold all the property he could to raise his share. Others, however, would give nothing while Stephen left Signe's money untouched. They thought Stephen asked them to give everything, while he kept something himself to fall back on.

At last Stephen went to Signe and asked her to sell her shop and other property so to pay for soldiers. He said, "You've been no fit wife to me for a long time; now you've the chance to make up for all that."

Signe replied, "I wonder if you remember the paper you signed when we married. I've not forgotten it, in any case, nor the way you've treated our son and kept our marriage vows. I won't help you now."

"As I see the law," said Stephen, "what is yours is mine in time of need."

"I know nothing of that. But this I can tell you, that your signed promise is safe with me."

Stephen hit Signe atop the head with the flat of his hand. Signe said, "I'll remember that, too."

"Your pride and your property are all one," said Stephen. "I won't let the one or the other stop me from helping so many people who are poorer than you."

"Someone else may think you're the hand of justice. I think the best any captain can hope for is a bit of glory."

Signe visited Olivia and told her how things stood with Stephen. Olivia said, "What Stephen asks now is wrong. You can count on my help if things come desperate, though I'm not anxious to cross Stephen. I doubt if you and Stephen have finished fighting yet. I won't be surprised if you end up each taking what the other cares most for."

Signe went home. She buried all her most valuable things in a secret place. Within the week, Stephen came to her shop during the middle of the day. He brought ten men with him, armed with rifles, and said, "I've come to take what's mine by right, whatever you say."

Signe's shop clerks were no match for soldiers; she sent them home. Stephen took everything he wanted and brought Signe back to his cottage. He put her in the kitchen and said, "You've tried to put me in hot water with your stingy ways. Now you've earned a place with the pots yourself." It was then late June and warm in Wisconsin.

Many among Stephen's soldiers resented it that Signe had been so little willing to help. Others thought her a witch. Almost all wanted her held prisoner. Stephen gave in to their wishes; he mounted a guard over her door. But he put the least able men to the task.

Signe escaped. She was unwilling to leave her son Michael behind, however, and stayed long enough to find him and take him away as well.

Mother and son came to Olivia's late in the night. Olivia gave them food and money. She said to Signe, "You're a sister to me; it will be no happy thing to have you gone. But there's nothing in it for you to stand against Stephen and half Wisconsin now.

We can hope you find better welcome next year, when Stephen's war is over for good or ill."

Signe and Michael left for the west early that same morning. They meant to find Edvard in Puget Sound. Stephen, on the other hand, sold Signe's shop and everything else of hers he could find.

All this happened during Signe's sixth summer in America; Michael was then a year old and a half.

Signe Visits Edvard

Signe and Michael reached Olalla early in September. Edvard greeted them well, and was especially pleased with his nephew. He promised them a place to stay for the winter.

At this time, and for some years after, Edvard lived with the Order of the Sabbath Blessing. The order's lodging lies on an island near Olalla in Puget Sound. Few trees grow on the island itself, and most the land is given over to grazing sheep. The country roundabout is not so rich for farming as Wisconsin, but there are forests, mountains, and water in all directions. To the east one peak stands over all others; it marks the seasons for the monks, since the sun rises in a new place each day.

Signe and Michael wintered with Edvard and without incident. But as spring came, Edvard marked that Signe was restless. He said to her, "I don't know what you mean to do, but there's no need to waste time over it if you've made up your mind."

"I'd like to do something," said Signe, "but nothing seems promising." She did not want to stay on near Puget Sound; she had little feeling for the place and less money to make her way. She feared to recome Wisconsin in case Stephen might now be so strong that he could do her harm. And she thought that to go to Norway as things stood would mean to leave everything to Stephen without even a fight.

Edvard said, "The cautious thing is to wait here for news of Stephen." He looked at her for a moment and went on, "Still, there is a way to make it safe for you now, though I can't guarantee you anything good once you get to Wisconsin. The Order of the Sabbath Blessing is known over all America and feared as well. I can get the fathers to speak for you; no one will dare to prison you, not even in a marriage, if you go with their blessing."

"That's a better idea than to stay a year here and quite likely to know no more at the end of it. Beside, it might be my turn to benefit from the law."

"I thought you might feel that way," said Edvard. "I'll come with you and speak for you, if you like. Perhaps Olivia will help us as well, even if she doesn't like to speak openly."

"You are more than kind to me in all this," said Signe. "You can be sure that I'll do no less for you someday."

Edvard arranged to leave the monastery for the summer. He also asked the fathers to give Signe their peace for her travels in the coming year.

The Suit Is Laid

Little is told of Stephen's campaign against the God-fearers, beyond that victories followed him in plenty. It is said that land-lords over all Wisconsin fell before him, that many died, and that Stephen himself killed the strongest of his foes.

But Stephen thought the victories incomplete, and that his later plans had been trayed to his enemies. They always had time to prepare for him, or else to flee. Stephen thought there must have been a spy among his officers.

Whatever is the truth of that, it is certain that Stephen gained a good deal of plunder for himself, and without having to stint his troops on the way. Some people have it that Stephen was well on the way to coming the highest man in Wisconsin, counting even the Primate Jeremy.

• • •

Signe and Edvard came to Olivia's house in the middle of June. They told her that they meant to sue for Signe's divorce from Stephen if there seemed a chance they might fare well in the courts.

Olivia in her turn told them of Stephen's exploits in the fall and said, "I think he's grown too strong for anyone's good; he's cruel to his enemies and proud to his friends, aside from the soldiers. I won't be surprised if he's brought down one way or another before long. At any rate, I'd like you to stay with me, if only so that Stephen will see that I count my friends highly."

Edvard said, "We can hardly stand against Stephen if he's as strong as you say. Why bring danger to you for nothing?"

"Many others will say the same," replied Olivia. "But great power makes great enemies. I've also heard this, that Stephen is beloved of all those who are used to being trod underfoot, but is feared by all the others. Most of all they fear that he may believe what he says."

"Even so," said Signe, "Stephen's a ruthless man; many a judge would rule for him as quickly from fear as for love."

"That may be true," said Olivia. "But there is a man who must stand against him—that's the Primate Jeremy. Were I in your place, I'd go to Kenosha and ask him to hear the case himself."

By this time, Stephen had heard of Signe's return and guessed what she meant to do. He sought out that Walter who had helped him in the summer of the Green Bay riots. The two men talked the matter over for some time. At last, Stephen said, "I don't see how these people can hope to stand against me, when they're no more than foreigners and fugitives."

But Walter said, "I think you forget that your own sister sides with them. Perhaps many others will do the same."

Stephen thought about this for a moment and then said, "Still, there's only one thing really to fear, and that's that Jeremy has turned against me once more, now that I've done all he asked.

But if that happens, I want him to bear the full weight of the thing himself."

Both Walter and Edvard now came to Kenosha and asked Jeremy to hear the case in person. Edvard said, "We have to face a man who's now the strongest in all Wisconsin, aside from you. We ask you to hear the case because you're the only one who can give a fair verdict."

Walter said that Jeremy might as well hear the case in the first place, "because the loser will have to call for you anyway."

Jeremy promised to give the matter his closest thought.

In the end, however, Jeremy did not hear the case, but let the honor fall to Bishop Frederick of Ripon. Whether this was good for one side or the other, no one could say.

The Trial

The time for the trial now comes. Stephen came first to Kenosha with Walter and a guard of forty men. Signe followed with Edvard and Olivia at her side.

Bishop Frederick opened his court in this way: "Deeply respected friends, we ask blessing on this ground in God's holy name, and by the power of the Trinity, passed to us here sitting by God's highest vicar in the land, the Primate Jeremy Smithson. Let all words that pass here be truth without reserve or color; let all who bear witness falsely take their sin to the grave and there find everlasting ground to repent.

"I see many people gathered here in the sight of God Almighty to witness our work. May you keep a true record in your hearts of all that passes here, so to speak it even should all writing fail.

"Hear now the first plea of Signe the Africa-born."

* * *

Edvard rose and faced the court. He said, "Our place must seem a poor one when we stand against the proudest man in Wisconsin and, as well, the army that serves him. Poor also is my untrained tongue when matched against that of a gifted lawyer. How great then must Stephen's offense be if we find no choice but to sue against him, even on these terms.

"Hear then our charges:

"For the first, Stephen the Captain has not kept his wife's bed at night, nor given her the affection and respect due her. So openly has he scorned her that no one fears to say evil of her, even in his presence.

"For the second: Stephen had threatened his lawful wife Signe with beating and other blood taunts; he has once made her a captive by force.

"For third: Stephen has trayed his own freely given word not to touch Signe's private wealth." Here Edvard gave Frederick the paper Signe had saved with Stephen's signature.

"For the last: Stephen has spoken ill of Michael, his son with Signe, and has neglected even the most urgent of father duties.

"For all these things we say it that Stephen is no fit husband."

Edvard called witnesses who spoke to all these points. Then he said, "By the laws of Wisconsin, we ask that this marriage be broken, and that Signe be freed of all blame in the matter."

Frederick asked Walter what he would say to all this on Stephen's behalf. Walter replied, "We'd rather not argue with a harlot, but save our words for the case against her."

Frederick said, "Hear then the first plea of Stephen the Captain."

Walter rose once more. "I stand here for a man who is well known to you all for his valor and his help to the unlucky. Of all those here, his wife Signe has the best reason to know his kindness. She came to our land with only those you see around her for company, near to winter and bereft of a roof. Stephen gave her shelter, and for her brother as well. In the spring Stephen found for her the shop she used for her own gain afterward. In the end, he gave her even himself, the finest gift a woman in Wisconsin could hope to have. It is a scandal that such a woman can stand here now and speak in bitterness against the man who's given her everything.

"Hear then our charges:

"Signe Africa-born is a harlot. She sported herself for a full winter with the foreigner Olav and never troubled to hide her deeds even in Stephen's presence. Signe is a whore and no fit wife.

"Again: Signe has taken to herself what was Stephen's by right, despite his pressing need and direct order. It is true that Stephen signed a paper; but we say that no paper can stand above the marriage oaths and the clear intent of the church.

"Again: Signe Africa-born left Stephen in August last and has kept herself from him from that time to this. This she did, though they were husband and housewoman before law and God.

"And once more: Signe kidnapped Stephen's son Michael and carried him with her on her flight; she has thought to harden Michael's mind against his father for all that time.

"For all these reasons, Signe is no fit wife to any man."

Witnesses spoke to the truth of the various charges; then Walter also asked that the marriage be broken and his client freed of blame.

Most people in the court thought the case had been evenly argued and that much would rest with the judge.

Frederick asked for second pleas.

Edvard rose and said, "We say that the hearing will be justly settled in this way:

"First, the divorce of Stephen and Signe should be granted, with no marriage duties spared.

"In the matter of property, Signe should be granted the money reserved to her by contract, and also half of what is left after that. This is a total of sixty thousand dollars.

"Third, the boy Michael must live with his mother as a matter of right.

"We ask nothing beyond these things, since the fame and valor of Stephen will not let us press further, whatever is right."

Walter then stood and spoke for Stephen: "We agree with Edvard on one thing only, that the divorce should be granted.

"But for money, we say that Signe left Wisconsin in August and has foregone all gains made since. We agree that she would normally be titled to half the joint wealth at the time she left, or a total of fifteen thousand dollars. But from this must be taken something to pay for the hardship caused Stephen by her absence. We say that a fair price for that would be eight thousand dollars.

"No man would take a child from its mother forever, even from so wretched a one as this. We ask that Micheal should live with his father for three months the year, but that he stay with Signe the rest of the time."

Walter sat back, and Frederick spoke, "By the grace of God, I call an end to the pleas in this case. Court returns at the morning to say judgment."

On the morning following, the court sat once more. Frederick came to his place with a roll of paper. He said, "I have thought long on this case, and with many prayers for guidance. Hear then the words of the court rendered by God through me, the chosen voice of His church."

He unrolled the paper and read:

"By the charge of the church and the special choice of Jeremy Smithson, Primate of Wisconsin, I, Frederick, hearing all witness and being of sound mind, render this word in the matter of Signe Africa-born and Stephen the Captain:

"The divorce of these two is granted; each is now a separate and whole person, with no duty to the other. The court makes no judgment of guilt in this matter.

"In the case of money, Signe Africa-born is in clear title to ten thousand dollars by signed first agreement. Of the further twenty thousand dollars existing last July, each partner is titled to half a share. All gains since then have followed from and depended on Stephen's illegal seizure of Signe's title, and were therefore gotten at her risk and without her consent. In law, all such gains belong to Signe, and are in the amount of eighty thousand dollars.

'Further, the characters of Stephen and Signe are such that it is unwise for them to live both in Wisconsin. Stephen has the longer standing in our land, and Signe is well shown of a willingness to live elsewhere. Therefore, Signe Africa-born is banished from this land at a time starting ninety days from today.

"Finally, I find Stephen's request for time to see his son both rightful and compelling. The court has no way to force Signe to give up the child once she is in exile, however. Therefore, Micheal is given in sole charge to his father Stephen, so to ensure that Stephen's request for three months in the year is met.

"So say I. How say you all?"

The people in the court answered, "So say we all."

Frederick spoke again: "I fix my name to this writ, and over it the seal granted me by Jeremy, Primate of Wisconsin." He wrote on the paper, fixed the seal, and rolled it up. "God's will being done, court ends."

Jeremy's Word

Signe listened to this verdict, and her face showed no expression. She left the court and said to Olivia, "They've made me sell my son." Olivia said nothing in reply; Signe turned and wept.

Stephen's face was grim; he said nothing at all.

Both sides appealed to Jeremy. Edvard claimed that the court had surpassed itself on two counts: first that it sent Micheal to live with Stephen for all time, when no one had asked more than three months in the year; and second that Signe was a ward of the Order of the Sabbath Blessing, and her natural children should come under the same protection.

Walter did not dispute these claims of Edvard's but said that the court had no right to give Signe one hundred thousand dollars when she had asked for no more than sixty thousand.

Jeremy pondered these arguments while the lawyers went back to Spring Green. At length he wrote his decision and sent it by letter to Edvard and Walter. It said:

Gentlemen:

Our church knows that God may speak through the mouth of any devout servant. It is therefore that we grant our judges a wide range of speaking and hesitate to overturn their verdicts, for we know also that he speaks best who has heard all the witness of a case.

The judgment in this case is unusual, but it is not in error. I have not the power to overturn it.

The court has granted no more than Stephen's request to see his son for three months in the year; it required the rest only because the court has the duty to ensure that its words can be enforced.

Nor is Michael a ward of the Order of the Sabbath Blessing; the order has mentioned only Signe; it could quite easily have mentioned Michael as well, had it meant to. The wardship would extend at most to a child of Signe's born after she was made a ward.

Finally, the court was within right to assign to Signe more property than she asked. A court may always do such a thing, in case that one side dare not assert its full claims, or fail to understand them. What a suit asks of the court in no way changes what justice demands of it.

Frederick's judgment stands as written. He has acted purely within the law, and with no sign of mental frailty.

This word is the final one.

                              Jeremy Smithson, Primate

Jeremy added a note to his letter. It read, "I fear the parties to this case may try to evade God's will by some subterfuge or other. The church will not shrink from asking its many friends in Spring Green to help guard against any breach of faith."

Jeremy also announced at about this time that Bishop Frederick's time as a judge was at an end. He granted Frederick a pension, rather larger than usual, and a house, in remembrance of the bishop's many years of service to God.

Signe Leaves Wisconsin

When Signe read Jeremy's decision, she said to Olivia, "It seems I'm not meant to live as other women." She then wrote this letter for Michael:

My son,

No one stands higher in my heart than you who are named for my father. I cannot see how your life or mine may go, but this word I give you, that a bed in Norway is yours and a seat of honor, if yet I live.

Leaving you is no choice of mine, as now you should know. Wherever your future may lie, you bring me a joy that stays by me still.

Signe

Signe also dug up all the things she had buried the year before. She packed some of these away for her trip to Norway, but brought most of them to Olivia along with the letter. Signe asked her friend to give Michael whatever he might need over the next years, but to save the letter to give him on his sixteenth birthday.

Olivia agreed to look after Michael in case Stephen did not. But she also said, "If I know my brother, he'll be a wiser man now than he was."

"And poorer," said Signe. She went on, "I owe a great debt

to you and also to Edvard. You can have as much of my money as you like, though I can't say it seems much of a gift."

Olivia replied, "It wouldn't be wise for me to take something Stephen thinks belongs to him. In any case, I'd rather have nothing to do with this money of yours; I've had a dream of it.

"It seemed to me that I saw you walking outside in the dawn, down where the riverbank is sandy and with many trees overhanging it. Then an old hag of a woman came into sight as well, a bit up the river from you. She was even uglier than most of the crones one hears of, with three warts on the chin and greenish eyebrows. At any rate, she came up to where you stood and spoke in a loud voice, saying, 'It's my wish to ride your back all the days you have yet to live.'

"Then she laughed and showed her teeth. They were mostly blackened, but there was a gleam of light from one of them. She said, 'Perhaps I'll make it worth your while, though; whoever gets me gets my golden tooth as well.'

"At that, she gave a full cackle and showed her teeth for a longer time. The golden tooth was now clear to see, and also the maggots in the gum underneath."

Signe listened to this dream and said, "That's certainly not the tale to cheer me on my way."

"No. But you might take it for warning that this treasure of yours is likely to bring great misfortune on someone."

"It's not pleased me up to now," said Signe.

Signe and Edvard now parted. Edvard was bound back to Olalla. He said, "I think it a fine thing that we part as better friends this time than last."

Signe said, "You've been kind and more than kind to me this past year, and it's a hard thing to watch you leave. Still, I hope your Christ-hardness doesn't lead you into trouble someday."

"We shall certainly hope that I'm more careful about things than you are," said Edvard and laughed.

Signe did not laugh, but gave Edvard the box of dominoes from Ragnhild and said, "I can't tell when we'll meet again. But let us make these a promise to keep each other in mind, even when we're far from sight."

Edvard took the box and said, "Keep me a place warm in Norway, and I'll do the same for you here."

Edvard left for the west the next day. But Signe gathered up all that she meant to take to Norway and went east, lake and river bound for the sea. It was near the end of August at this time.

Signe Cures a Child

Signe stopped the night at an inn on the eighth day of her journey. A woman called Joan also stayed there, and as well her daughter Margaret. Joan had been born in Canada, a blond-haired woman of middle height. The daughter was six winters old, and taken up by illness for some days past. Priests had come and a doctor, but she came no better for all of that. Joan broke her travel for Margaret's sake. But she was without cheer; she looked for only the worst to happen.

The Norsewoman and the Canadian came to talk and soon spoke of the sick child. After a time, Signe said, "I've learned something of these matters. Perhaps you'd like me to look at your daughter; it's possible the doctor's not done the right things by her."

Joan agreed to show Signe her daughter; the women went to the girl's bed; she lay in the bed in a sweat, with her hair yellow and lank on the pillow. Signe saw a chart on the wall and read on it all the treatment that had been given up to then.

Signe said, "You will know best how you like the look of this doctor, but it's my guess he knows little about his business." She looked at the child with care and asked Joan closely how the illness had taken hold and how it had run afterwards. Then she said, "I can give something that might help her, if you like."

Joan saw nothing to lose, since neither priest nor doctor had done much up to then. The Canadian went to get the four herbs that Signe asked, along with a bowl to grind them in and some clean water. Signe stayed with Margaret, who said nothing but groaned from time to time.

Joan returned. Signe thanked her for the herbs and said, "Now you must leave me in peace with Margaret, and I will watch her through the night. Come back with the morning, and we'll see if things haven't turned for the better."

Joan left. Signe ground the herbs together and mixed them in the water. She fed the whole thing to Margaret and marked on the chart all that she did. Signe then sat by Margaret's side and sang to her till she slept. Signe stayed the whole of the night. The fever broke soon before daylight. Both Signe and Margaret slept quietly after that, the Norsewoman on her chair.

Joan found both doctor and patient still asleep when she came back at breakfast time. Margaret was easily roused and hungry. But it took some time to wake Signe. Signe soon left Margaret and Joan together and went off to look after other things.

The doctor came with the afternoon. He looked at his chart and then at Margaret. He said, "It's a lucky thing that this old wives' cure got so little in the way of my own work. Still, the girl's tough as an ox underneath; she was bound to come well in the end, whatever was done to her."

Signe stayed in the inn with Joan and Margaret for three days more. By then, Margaret had come almost well. She was also a great favorite of Signe's.

The time now came for Signe to travel on to the east. Joan said, "There's no need to go so far when you can find bed and hearth with us for the winter."

Signe thought on this for a time; the season was late. At last she said, "A thousand thanks shall you have, but I still hope to reach Norway before the winter."

"We should like to repay our debt to you," said Joan.

"It's I who owe you," replied Signe, "for letting me to show my skill. It's enough to see a child with her mother again."

Signe left and traveled east. No more is told of her journey until she reached the ocean and boarded the last ship bound over the sea for that year.

Signe in Iceland

Signe's ship stopped first at Iceland to trade wood for wool and fish. Signe came ashore and fared east to a place near Skogafoss where once her mother had lived. Before she reached that place, however, she came to a hollow that was somewhat sheltered from the wind. Inside the hollow were about fifteen huts, all quite ramshackle and difficult to see in the snow. Signe looked around the huts for a time and could find no one in the settlement, though the huts showed signs of being lived in still.

Signe now climbed one side the hollow. A man came to stand atop the rocks. He spoke in English and said, "Get your Icelandic face off from here and leave our houses as they stand."

Signe replied, also in English, "Perhaps these Icelanders of yours are better at bearing orders than I."

"Whatever you are, there's little good that can come from you. All we want is for you to go off, and the sooner the better."

Signe said nothing but stayed standing where she was.

The man said, "What must you have from us to leave?"

"The story of how English tongues are found in this place, for a start."

"That I can give you," said the man, "since talk is cheap. But then you must go away and not come back. Or else you must be a witch and bring us our wish."

"That's fair enough," said Signe.

The man came down next to Signe. He told this story: "My name is Ralph. My people came here from Canada some years ago. We stayed in New Brunswick for the first years after the war, living mostly by fishing and taking up what the old people left behind. We were more than a hundred people in those days.

"But one year, some soldiers came from the south. They took both our good boats and our land. They said we could stay and work as tenants on our old land. Or else we could sail off in some smaller boats they didn't need. Most of us chose to leave.

"We sailed north along the coast, because we feared the sickness further south. We tried to land in one place, but the people there drove us back into the sea. At last we came to another place where we could do the chasing, and there we wintered.

"The natives came back with the spring, however, and in greater numbers than before. Many of us died trying to fight them off, but we lost even so. The rest of us put out to sea in three boats. One of them reached this land, and eighteen people with it. But we say nothing of the others.

"The Icelanders would have nothing to do with us at first. After a time, though, they came to fear that we might carry disease; they put us in jail for a time, and then found this land for us to live on. But even now they take most of our wealth each year in taxes. They also come to watch us; they laugh because we do things strangely to their eyes, and have no money. They even bring Africans to look at us now."

Ralph stopped and would say no more. So Signe said, "One could almost think you wish for money. But I'd be careful of that, if I were you."

Ralph replied, "We hope for many things, and money would get us most of them."

Signe left as she promised and went on to Skogafoss.

●   ●   ●

Signe soon recame Reykjavik. She put half her treasure into a double chest and took it out into the country where the Canadians lived. The houses were as empty as before when she came there. Signe poured the money out onto the ground in the middle of the village and then went up into the rocks to find Ralph.

That man came out onto the top of the rocks and said, "Why do you break your word and come back to us?"

"I'm no liar," said Signe, "and your wish lies answered below."

"How is that?"

"I've brought you money in metal coin, and more than you looked to see, I think. It hasn't done me any good, but it could be that you'll have better luck from it. Still, if I had it to guess, I'd say that you won't end up splitting it evenly."

"That's more our worry than yours, now."

"Then everything's as you wished it," said Signe, "and I'm free of a haunting hag."

Signe left and went south from the village. But she stopped near enough to the huts to see what the Canadians might do.

The villagers came down to their huts and saw the treasure. They shouted and laughed at first, and poured the coins over each other's heads. But before long, one person and another came to pocket a coin here and there. They soon came to fight each the other; they left three corpses to feed the ravens by the end of the day.

Signe moved on and camped further to the south.

A man came to Signe's camp near to daylight the next morning. She slept in blankets, but was wakeful at that time and saw that the man was Ralph. He had a knife in one hand.

The man came up to Signe and seemed ready to stab her dead. But Signe rolled under his arm as he stabbed at her and hit him full in the stomach. The blow knocked Ralph's breath away, and he dropped his knife. Signe picked the weapon up and said, "What do you mean to do?"

Ralph could say nothing for a time, and then, "Your money is full of the devil, every bit of it, and you must have known that, or you'd never have given it us. It's only right if we try to repay you as you deserve."

"You're the ones who are cursed when you use the money in such a way, not I who only brought you what you asked."

Ralph said, "I didn't think I could do much against a witch like you, but the others said I had to try. Now they're like to try me."

Signe set herself to leave. There was a cliff nearby, too high to jump, but easy enough to climb down. She threw the knife over it and said, "I'm no witch, and you're no fool. Kill a sheep in my place."

Signe came back to Reykjavik; she had not long to wait for her ship on to Norway.

❄ Part Three
Norway

Introduction

Europe in Signe's day was for the most part even poorer than North America—largely as a result of the interdict placed on it by the Organization of African Unity in 13 M.E. This interdict, designed to prevent African conflict over European spoils, severely restricted trade between Europe and the rest of the world by limiting the tonnage of ships and by forbidding any non-European ship from berthing longer than three days in a European port. It also prohibited the establishment of any industry or colony on the continent.

The African interdict was broken occasionally, but it was effective enough to leave Europe as little more than a series of isolated peasant communities. The result could be catastrophic when, for instance, a local famine could not be alleviated by the purchase of grain from other places.

Norway was relatively prosperous in these years. Like other peripheral countries (Ireland, Portugal), she was less affected by the war than most. The long tradition of seafaring allowed western Norway in particular to supplement a rather meager subsistence-farming economy with both fishing and what overseas trade could be found. But relative prosperity in first-century Europe still meant substantial, even desperate, privation by prewar standards.

Most of western Norway was governed by popular assemblies

(called Things), which served both to make laws and to judge court cases. They were generally made up of all citizens (with some restrictions based on the length of residence). As might be expected, however, the wealthy and well-connected often exercised a power beyond their numbers.

A typical Thing would rule for one of the major fjords, or for up to several hundred miles of outer coastal lands. Although each Thing was nominally independent, there appears to have been considerable diplomatic activity among them, leading to large-scale trading agreements and to some effort to harmonize the laws of the various Things.

In early times, west Norway also displayed substantial equality between men and women: both were allowed to speak on an equal footing at the Thing; a woman's property rights were guaranteed in marriage; men and women had equal rights in divorce.

In later years there was an erosion of the rights and powers of women. By 30 M.E. it was already rare for a woman to speak at the Thing; in 64 M.E. women lost the right to vote; and after 73 M.E. they lost the right to speak altogether. Some scholars speculate that Signe's Saying may be the work of a woman who saw little merit in the political practice of her day.

Mention should be made of a curious aspect of Norwegian life in these years: the prohibition of firearms. Things over most of Norway passed laws making it illegal to own a firearm of any kind, as one of them says in a note appended to the law, "so that people may have a chance to survive their quarrels."

Signe Arrives in Norway

The story now turns to the time when Signe Ragnhilds-datter came home to Norway.

The ship from Iceland stopped at Haugesund, which was then the greatest town of the Fjordlands. But Signe held on to Hardanger in a boat belonging to Stein Larsson, that same Stein who lived in Odda and was called the Dancer. Stein told Signe how

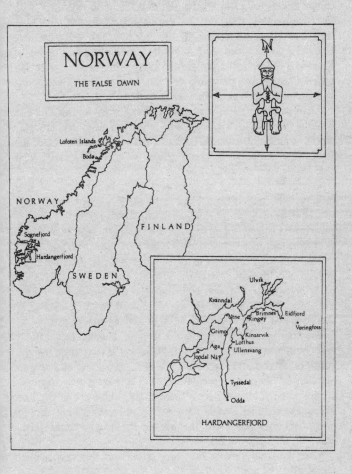

NORWAY

THE FALSE DAWN

NORWAY

Lofoten Islands
Bodø

Sognefjord
Hardangerfjord

SWEDEN

FINLAND

Ulvik
Kvanndal
Utne   Brimnes   Eidfjord
Ringøy
Grimo   Kinsarvik   Vøringfoss
Aga   Lofthus
Jondal   Nå   Ullensvang
Tyssedal
Odda

HARDANGERFJORD

things stood for her in Hardanger: that Ragnhild lived still with Per Scarmouth in Eidfjord; that Per's son Ulf stayed at Utne with his friend Olav Whitebrow, the Southlander; that Ulf's brother, Einar Pers-son, lived with his wife Gunilla Auduns-datter at Kvanndal. Einar and Gunilla had living with them a foster son called Gustav, but only two of their own children lived, sons called Helgi and Bjorn. They were both very young.

Stein said that there was an interesting story told of Gustav, Einar's foster son. The boy was already sixteen winters old, though small for his years. He had a red mark on one side of his face, which covered all of one cheek; he tried not to show that side of his face most the time.

Gustav's father had been named Karl; he was one of two brothers who traded from Flam in Sognefjord. Karl took goods overland from Sogn to Hardanger; his brother Torkjell usually captained a ship to the north. All the family thought themselves Christians but said fewer prayers than they thought right.

Karl came to Hardanger in the summer of the year before Signe arrived and brought Gustave with him. One night Karl played cards with Einar and won from him the promise of two horses to help recome Sogn later in the year. Karl fell sick soon after that, however, and could not think of leaving till the fall.

But Karl came sicker still in the autumn. He then called Einar and Gunilla to see him and said, "I think I'll have little use for your horses as things stand, but you have something of a debt to me even so. Perhaps we could settle it this way, that you take Gustav to be your foster son. You can give him work as you like during the summer, but in the winter you must let him learn to priest. It's my fondest wish that my son should be a better Christian than his father or his uncle."

Einar was not sure at first how to answer this proposal; it seemed that he and Gunilla might be too young to foster so old a boy. But Gunilla thought the idea an excellent one and accepted at once. Karl died a bit later, and Gustav came to live at Kvanndal. He was by now thought a cheerful lad and hardworking. Both

Einar and Gunilla were said to give him one small thing or another from time to time.

Signe listened to this story and to everything else that Stein could tell her of Hardanger. At the last, she asked to go ashore at Utne, "for that seems as likely as any place to hold a friend."

Signe found her way up from the dock at Utne to Ulf's house with Olav, which lay some way uphill from the churchyard. Ulf met her at the house and soon learned who she was. He said, "I've often thought of meeting you, my cousin, and no less after what Olav's said of you."

Signe replied, "I'm glad for your welcome, and also to find a part my family." She asked after Olav, whether he might be near to hand.

"As to that," said Ulf, "your luck is mixed. He's been north for the season. But the days will be short and snowdust there by now, so we look to see his sail any day."

Signe said, "I've traveled long enough to be weary. Still, I hoped to see Olav before the winter."

"Then you must stay here in this house of ours until he comes. He'd take it badly if you left before then, in any case, if he means what he's said of you."

Signe agreed to stay and settled to live in the front room of Ulf's house.

Einar, Gunilla, and Olav

But the first to come to Utne were not Olav, but Einar Pers-son and Gunilla. They brought a well-smoked lamb with them but left Gustav behind to watch for his foster brothers, Helgi and Bjorn.

Einar and Gunilla found both Signe and Ulf at home. Einar seemed surprised to see Signe; he said to Ulf, "I wonder who this guest of yours can be; she looks very like one of our own family, though the hair's not so light as yours."

Ulf replied, "This is Signe who's come from America and from Africa before that. She might well have the family look, since she's Aunt Ragnhild's daughter."

Einar and Gunilla made something of a show to welcome Signe. Then Gunilla said to Ulf, "We brought this lamb over to you for your birthday, but it might be better still if we made it up for a family dinner here and now. We can bring you another later on."

Ulf replied, "Let's eat it today by all means. I've not feasted my guest very well as yet. And there's no need to bring another, if you'd not thought to lose two."

Einar and Gunilla talked with Signe while Ulf worked at the fire. The conversation went well enough at first. After a time, Einar asked Signe what had brought her to Hardanger. He had heard that she was married in America, and had a son there.

Signe told some of what had fallen her in America and that the court had sent her off from Wisconsin, whatever she might think of the matter. She said, "As for coming here, it seemed better to come to the land that bore my mother than to a place I know nothing of."

Einar replied, "Perhaps you have done the best thing. Still, we don't often think highly of a woman who's left her husband."

But Gunilla spoke next, "You can't judge an outlander as quickly as a neighbor, Einar." To Signe she said, "Even so, it must have been a hard choice, leaving your son so far behind."

Ulf now asked his guests to dinner. At the meal, Einar spoke again to Signe and asked which religion she held to. Signe replied that she preferred that god who promised her the best luck, or else to believe in none at all. The Kvanndalers laughed at that. Gunilla said, "It's easy to see that Miss Signe's a clever girl."

After dinner, everyone recame the front room; that was the place used both for conversation and to lodge guests. Ulf, Einar, and Gunilla sat down and began to talk. But Signe said she was tired from her trip. She lay down to one side of the room.

Before long, Signe seemed well asleep. Gunilla now said to Ulf, "This cousin of yours is more than a bit proud, is she not?"

"She hasn't struck me so up to now," said Ulf.

"Still, you're a patient man to put up with her."

Einar spoke to his brother next and said, "What will you do with her when Olav comes? He's got no duty to like her."

"No," said Ulf, "but he might have his own thoughts about her, even so."

But Gunilla had long admired Olav. She said, "I'm sure he'll be able to see what you won't, Ulf, that she's a selfish girl and bound to cause trouble."

Ulf replied, "I can't complain when you say just what you think. Still, you deal badly with my guest."

The Kvanndalers left in the morning. Einar told Signe, "It's too bad you can't come across the fjord to visit with us. Still, I can see how much you want to get home to see your mother."

And Gunilla said, "You're sure to like Norway, when you learn to hear what's left unsaid."

Olav came to Utne in the afternoon of the sixth day that Signe stayed there. He saw her clothes in the front room and called to Ulf, asking where their guest might be.

Ulf joined Olav and said, "I'm surprised you're so eager to meet this passing traveler of ours."

"She's more than that to me," said Olav, "and well you know it."

Signe came into the room at that. She had been working outside. She and Olav greeted each other as more than friends. Olav said, "I feared not to see you again. I can hope we won't be so long parted again."

"That's a hope we share, then," replied Signe. Olav smiled widely at these words. Signe went on, "But I'd call that woman stupid who went from one husband to another in a single year."

"Yes, well," said Olav, "there is time left yet in the three years I promised you. Still, you can't stop me from being glad in you now."

"No," said Signe Ragnhilds-datter, "that I cannot."

Signe stayed three days longer with Ulf and Olav before going on to her mother's farm at Eidfjord. There she wintered in a small hut of her own. Once in the winter, Inger Arnes-datter, Ragnhild's sister who had lived many years in the mountains, came down to Eidfjord. There was a fast friendship between Signe and Inger.

At Inger's

Near to midsummer of the year following, Signe traveled up to Inger's stead. She planned to stay for two weeks, or as long after that as seemed wise. She brought presents with her and useful things for the year, and said to Inger, "I'm far from doubting that you can make your own way, you who've lived here so long. Still, it's best to honor one's family when one can."

Inger made no reply, but seemed happy enough to smoke a pipe of Signe's tobacco in the evening. During the days, Inger and Signe worked together at one thing and another, both in Inger's hut and in the fields beyond.

So things went for some time. One day, however, five men came to Inger's stead from the east. They were poorly clad and looked none too well fed either. Their leader was a slight man and young, and stooped in the shoulder. He called himself Jesu.

Jesu and his men said they were Christians and had fled their homes east of the Vidda when some Africans came. "Those people wanted us to work only for them and not for God," said Jesu.

Inger listened to this story and asked, "What would you have from me?"

"Only a place to sleep," said Jesu, "and perhaps some food to help us on the way to a new land."

Inger looked from one man to the next and said, "These mountains are poorer than you think and older. Sleep in the stable if you like; or not, if it's too poor."

Jesu and his friends went to the barn. Signe said to Inger, "These are hardly the people one would choose for guests."

"No," said the aunt, "but I won't refuse simple things in a hard world, either."

Jesu and his men recame Inger's hut late in the day. Inger gave them potatoes to eat, as many as they liked. Then one man, called Lukas, said, "You've given us a bed and a meal, and that's more than we had this morning. Still, you've fed us no meat, you who have so many sheep and cows."

Signe said, "It's a poor thing to complain of food you've done nothing to earn."

And Inger said, "It's just as well in any case. The animals here filled their meat with poison during the bad times, so people would eat fewer of them. Even now, a visitor to the fjords can come to grief over a rib of beef."

Pal said, "I think you're lying."

Inger shrugged. But Signe rose and poured a glass of ale over Pal's head. It looked as if Pal might start a fight then and there. But Jesu spoke first. "Come, brothers, let us sleep. Tomorrow will be time enough for other things."

The next day, the Christians asked for meat once more. Each man carried a knife. Inger thought it best to agree to their requests.

Signe soon said to Inger, "Things are come to a bad pass when these people can make us do just what they want."

"So it seems," replied Inger. "Still, I doubt they've thought of everything." She asked Signe to put some salt beef in the cooking pot. She herself went outside and some way up the fell. Inger soon recame the house with some small green-black leaves. She put half of these into the pot with the salt beef and put the rest aside for another time.

The five pilgrims had little good to say about the idea of salt beef, and even less once they tasted it. Jan said, "You must think us paltry folk if this is the best you'll do."

"On the contrary," said Inger, "only the best people come so far into the mountains. As for the beef, the salt kills some of the poison. I'd not like the work of burying you."

Pal said, "We'll eat this tonight since there's not much choice. But we can kill a sheep as well as you in the morning."

Signe and Inger ate little, but the five Christians ate as well as on the night before. They recame the barn in high spirits. But after a short time, each of them fell ill. Their stomachs were most affected, but their faces went a bit green as well.

Per said, "This Inger's a mean sort of woman."

The next day, Jesu's third at Inger's stead, the men killed a lamb on their own. They spitted the lamb and cooked it over an open fire, and basted it from time to time with ale, as was the custom in those days.

Per said, "Those women won't fool us so easily a second time." But the truth was that Inger had put the rest of her plants in with the ale.

When the meal was ready, Signe and Inger would have none of it. "Even for us, it would go badly to eat a lamb so fresh," said Signe. "What you have there would kill a mountain troll."

"More for us, then," said Pal. Jesu and his men ate their fill a third time. Before long, the illness broke over them once more, and even less kindly than before. They found it difficult to recome their beds for the night.

Jesu came to Inger in the morning and said, "It seems that God means us for greater things than to stay here."

Inger asked the men where they would go next. Jesu said they meant to go on to the fjordlands. Inger said, "I thought you might. Be careful of the berries there. Most people like them even less than the meat."

Jesu in Hardanger

Jesu and his disciples came down from Inger's fell and at last to Kinsarvik. There they stayed some days at the inn belonging to Ivar Eskils-son. Ivar thought it a great joke that his guests ate only beer and bread. But he liked it less when they had no money to pay him.

Ivar told them they must now leave. Jesu and his followers talked for some time and decided it was not good to continue down one road and up the next.

They left the inn and pitched their tent in a meadow overlooking Kinsarvik. There they stayed until fall. Then they had to come to the Thinghouse for the autumn Council, there to ask the right to stay in Hardanger a longer time.

Jesu told the Council how he and his men had journeyed from the east, and what had happened at Inger's stead and afterwards. He ended by saying, "Now we hope to stay here. There's no telling what might go wrong somewhere else, if the food's bad here."

Trygve the Lawspeaker asked if anyone wished to speak about this matter. Gunvald Vidals-priest was the first to rise. He was already an old man in those days, but well heeded in most things.

He reminded the Council that Jesu was not the first Christian to come from the east, and that some of the others had turned out to be thieves. "These men follow the old god, the one who died twice for our sins, once on the cross, as they say, and again, finally, at Ragnarok. Perhaps they mean well, these men; but whoever chooses a god so carelessly is likely to find bad fortune in the end."

Signe Ragnhilds-datter also spoke: "My friends, I have more reason than most to praise the warmth of your welcome. Even so, kindness isn't always wisdom. I know these men; we'll do better to deal with them as little as we can."

At these words, Einar Pers-son stood and said, "This Signe's almost as kind as her gracious mother. Why should we fear these fellows just for the god they follow? Many among us do the same. There's no need to toss them to the snow, at any rate; they can work a day for a day's bread here just as well."

No one answered these words, so Einar went on: "I see I must vouch for them myself, or no one will. Very well. I say it now before this Council and many other witnesses, that I shall take up these five lives, that so long as they keep to my land and do as is right for bondsmen, I shall look to their safety and make good their quarrels. So I swear."

Trygve said, "We must all think your words generous, Einar." He asked Jesu what answer he might have.

There seemed little chance that the Christians would find better treatment so late in the year. Jesu said, "We thank God that He has sent us a brother in our time of need. We accept this offer, and gratefully."

The Thingholder that year was Oddvar Eskils-son, the same who later married Helga the Gray and went to live in Grimo. He spoke these words, "By all law and custom, we of the Council agree to these terms as we have heard them."

Jesu and his men left the Council with Einar and went to live with him at Kvanndal. For some time all went well with this arrangement. But then Jesu refused to let his men work on saints' days or on the Sabbath, until there seemed hardly a day on which they did work willingly. Einar made them to work anyway; but the work made things worse rather than better as often as not. Jesu said it was God's will that their efforts should come to so little, if they had to do things on holy days.

Einar said, "Your god teaches poverty, if I recall it rightly. I won't be the one to tempt you." He gave them no more wood for fires, but let them use whatever brush they could find instead. But Jesu and his men still worked poorly or not at all. Once, Per said to Einar, "At least, cold hands are good for the soul, though they don't seem to help the hammer much." Einar thought these words a great insolence; but there was little he could do just then.

In the spring, however, Einar told Jesu that the time had come for his men to earn the keep they had gotten so cheaply up to now. The first thing for them to do was to go up to the summer pastures and see that the fences were in order.

Jesu made no objection to that. He and his men set off the next day. The days now passed, and Jesu was not seen again. Soon, Gunilla found one small thing and another missing from her house. She came more annoyed at each thing she missed and spared few of Einar's feelings in telling him just what she thought of his openhandedness.

Einar's Law

Einar brooded on all this. He came to the Thing at Kinsarvik that spring and proposed a law that no Christian be let to come into the land and practice that religion. Most people at the Thing were ready to take Einar's part in this; they thought that Jesu had given him a hard time.

But Einar was no great lawyer, and he framed his law somewhat carelessly when first he spoke it. Some priests of the new gods thought to use it to proscribe all Christians, even those who had always lived in Hardanger.

It was Gunvald Vidals-priest who proposed this. He asked also that those who practiced the old religion be tried by the new priests, in case there would otherwise be a long delay before the Thing or the Council met. And finally he asked that the penalty be whatever the judging court might decide, including even death. "For," said he, "these people are outlaws already as often as not."

Many Christians were present at the Thing. No one spoke against Gunvald for some time, though. People feared that their words might too easily turn against them later on.

At last, Einar's foster son, Gustav, went and spoke to his near-father. Einar then rose and said that he had no objection to most of what Gunvald said, but also that, "I would not have my law punish the innocent along with the guilty. Nothing in it should hinder those living in the fjordlands now from praying as they choose. And even those who come later should be let to speak as they like in private."

Several others spoke then, both for and against the law. Then Ulf Pers-son spoke: "Einar is a brother and dear to me. I do not speak against him lightly. But this law of his grows from fear and disappointment. It seeks what cannot be found—a way to save people from themselves. It's bad enough to have a pointless law, but I fear that this one will one day bring harm we can none of us foresee."

Soon after, the Thing divided. A third part of those present stood with Ulf, and five more beside. But the greater number went over to Einar's side, and his word became law.

Signe and Olav

At the end of the Thing, Olav asked Signe if he might come to Eidfjord before he set off for his summer trade. She answered that it was only right to welcome a friend when he wished to come. Olav agreed to come after a few days.

• • •

Signe recame home and told Ragnhild that Olav meant to come soon. Ragnhild said, "You bring only good news, since that man has always been a friend to this house."

But Signe said, "I doubt if the visit will go so easily as one could hope. He gave me a troth three years ago, and it's all come due this spring, one way or the other."

Ragnhild said, "That's the first you've said of the matter to me. But there's not much help for you, anyway, if it takes you three years to decide on a man like Olav."

"Yes, well. It may not be so hard a choice as that."

Olav came to Eidfjord. Ragnhild and Per gave him a full welcome, and Olav gave Ragnhild a package of several kinds of piano wire. He said, "I've heard that you love your piano over all things. But perhaps you can't so easily find string for it. I thought of you when I came across these, though I know nothing of tunes." Ragnhild came even warmer in her welcome after that, but Signe stayed somewhat distant.

Olav spoke with Signe later in the evening. He said, "I think you've not forgotten the promise I made to you in America. I've said nothing about it up to now, because there was still time to run. But now you should know that my heart's not changed since then; on the other hand, there's not much point to waiting an answer till I'm too old to use it. You must tell me plainly how you stand. Then I'll marry you or not as you like; but if not, I'll not ask it of you again."

Signe said, "There's no man I'd rather live with, Olav. But I fear they had it right in Wisconsin, those who said that I'm no fit wife to any man. My last marriage didn't turn out well, and I'm not about to be like other wives just to have a husband. It won't surprise me if you come disappointed in me before we're married long."

"I'm not sure what you mean to answer when you speak in

such a way," said Olav. "But I remember that once Stephen signed a paper in case things went bad. I can do that as well, if you like."

"Stephen's promises ended up little better than the marriage, as well you know. Still, it's likely you're more to be trusted on these things than most, and the laws here are more a help to me as well."

"It's a hopeful thing if you've looked into the law."

But now Signe said, "I've been married and not. Now I can do as I like, go where I'm called, and answer to no one. You can do all that as well. But when we marry, you'll go on in that way, and I'll be tied down every minute."

Olav replied, "I doubt any promise of mine will ease your mind on that count. On the other hand, you might trust yourself not to give in so far, given the way you've lived up to now."

"Let me think on it till morning."

Olav agreed to that and then went to his room in Ragnhild's house.

Signe rose early on the morning following. She got together chicken eggs, bread, jam, goat's cheese, and smoked fish, and took them all to Ragnhild's house. She made them into a breakfast and took them to Olav's room while the daylight was still quite pale, and before he was fully awake. She put a note under the plate which read, "Yes, and tomorrow you can serve me."

She went home again.

Olav ate his breakfast, rose, and went to walk along the fjord west of Eidfjord and south of the water for all the day. Farmers along his way saw that he stopped from time to time to dance a small jig. This was thought so extraordinary a sight that word came back to Signe. She thought a moment, and then grinned and said, "But I can't think he keeps time to the music."

Signe and Olav spoke together on the day following. They agreed to marry when Olav should come home from the south for the fall.

• • •

Gustav Karls-son finished his studies to be a priest of Christ in this summer also. But he then faced a difficult choice. The Christians of those days would not pay a man to priest until he had been tested five years. They thought in this way to be sure that priests knew something of the poverty of the world. But Gustav had little taste for being poor. At last he decided to recome Sognefjord, so to join his uncle Torkjell, who still traded in the north.

Gustav told Einar of his plans, but he also said, "You and Gunilla are my real family now; you can be sure to see me back in Hardanger when my days at sea are done."

Einar replied that nothing would please him or Gunilla better than that Gustav should think of Kvanndal as home.

The story now passes to the autumn when Olav's ship recame Hardanger. Signe met him at Utne, and the two talked of everything about their wedding. They were quickly at one on each point, save the question of who should come to the feast afterward. Signe was unwilling to show any friendship toward Einar or Gunilla. She said, "Those two have done nothing but insult me from my first days in Norway."

Olav said, "Yet Ulf is my greatest friend, and he's not much less to you. He won't come either if we insist on slighting his brother."

"That's up to him; Einar's coming is up to us."

But Signe gave in in the end, so that Einar and Gunilla were asked to be a part of the wedding, after all.

When Einar first heard that Signe and Olav were to marry, he said, "It can't be right for her to marry here when she still has another husband alive oversea." But he and Gunilla thought also that Signe was unlikely to live with Olav at Utne and at Eidfjord at the same time. This made them more cheerful, and they agreed to come.

• • •

All went well at the wedding. Einar and Gunilla came to the feast after, but found themselves sitting at the second table. All the rest of the family ate with the wedding pair.

Gunilla said, "This can only be Signe's doing. I don't think we should soon forgive her."

Einar agreed and said, "Still, there's not much else we could look for from a woman like that. It comes to me also that she's never given us a present for our wedding, though it was grander than this."

Signe and Olav lived in the house at Utne after the wedding. Ulf stayed there also off and then, but he spent many weeks in Ringoy at the farm of a man called Jan. Jan had a daughter called Britt of whom Ulf was fond.

Some time after the wedding feast, Signe missed a pair of silver candleholders that were a present from one of Olav's friends in the north. These candleholders were inlaid with most difficult patterns, and not the sort of things to be mislaid lightly.

Word came later that just such a pair of candlesticks was to be seen at Einar's house in Kvanndal. A week more passed, and there came a letter from Einar to his cousin Signe. The letter thanked Signe for her generous wedding gifts, even though they were a bit late in coming. Einar and Gunilla promised to take the candleholders in the spirit in which they had been given.

Signe came into a rage at this, and wanted to cross the fjord at once to recover the candlesticks by force, if need be. But no action of the sort was possible, because the Kvanndalers had more bondsmen and other friends who could be counted on for help. Olav said he would see if there was not some way to use the law to recover the candleholders.

Olav went to the Lawspeaker for the next Thing, a man called Tomas Gunnars-son, who lived in Brimnes. Olav told the Lawspeaker what had happened, and how insolently Einar had treated with them. Tomas said, "It's not easy to get things back once they're given. Even if you succeed, people speak badly of you. And everyone knows how openhanded Signe is; she'd be the first to give such a thing, and especially to a close cousin like Einar."

Tomas was a friend of Einar, and also in debt to him. Olav said no more, but came home to Signe and told her how things stood. She said, "I can see this isn't the sort of thing to fight any further. But it doesn't make Einar any dearer to me."

Olav and Signe Are Invited North

Early in the spring following, Lawspeaker Tomas came to Utne. By this time, Signe was with child. Tomas told Olav that Hardanger's man in the far north was dead; he asked Olav to go to Stamsund in the Lofoten Islands to place him.

Olav said, "That's a land without trees and dark in the winter."

"That's true," said Tomas. "On the other hand, it's rich in walrus tusk and African money."

"Little cause to live there," said Olav.

"They say also that a Scot has come there to buy against us fjordsmen. Many will thank the man who stops him."

"Yes," said Olav, "and it won't hurt you if I fail." But Olav agreed to talk with Signe about the matter.

In the evening, Olav told Signe what Tomas had in mind, and also that he was minded to go. Signe said, "I've nothing against this trip of yours. But I like it less that you think to leave me behind."

Olav replied that it might be a bad idea for Signe to travel just then. But Signe said, "All times will be bad if I listen to you. Either we can stay together here, safe from harm, or we can go together. If we do that, they must pay us half again as much as they did the last man, and in equal shares."

Olav said, "I see you won't be talked down from this. Still, it's no easy bargain to press with Tomas."

"It's a cheap price if they want help as badly as it sounds."

Olav told Tomas what Signe had said and added, "If we go, we must be able to make whatever bargain's needed, and the captains will have to live with it."

"You are a hard man," said Tomas, "and people will say you're a selfish pair."

"I've heard that in any case," said Olav. So the matter was settled. Signe and Olav were charged to set off as soon as they could.

This was also the spring that Ulf Pers-son married Britt Jans-datter. Signe and Olav left their share of the house at Utne to Britt and Ulf. Signe also sent a letter to Einar, her cousin. It was on top of a large box and said:

Greetings, cousin,

You've a fondness for candlesticks, I'm told. Here's something to burn in them, or else in your pipe.

Signe.

This box reached Einar on the day Signe and Olav left for the north. There were two cowpats inside. Einar said little about the present, but Gunilla took the matter badly. She said, "There's no end to that woman's insults."

In the North

Signe and Olav came to Stamsund well after the sun had turned, but before the spring was fully come to the far north.

They found that a Scot named Bruce was there before them.

Many fishermen and traders had already agreed to trade with the Scots.

Through the summer, Olav promised those who would sell to the fjordlanders that they could share in the profits of voyages to the south. Many larger traders thought this a fine idea; they were willing to risk more in the hope to gain more.

In the end, the trade was divided about in half between the Scots and the fjordlanders.

Among the fjordland ships that came north that summer was one called the *Gudvangen*. This ship came from Sognefjord and was captained by Torkjell, the uncle of Gustav Karls-son, the foster son of Einar.

Torkjell was little pleased that he stood to share his profit. He sent Gustav ashore to talk with Olav. Gustav asked Olav to lower the share the *Gudvangen* would have to pay the islanders, or else to let her trade as before. Gustav reminded Olav of how well they knew each the other and said, "It's no more than a matter of helping one's friends and family."

But Olav replied, "I've more friends than you alone, and many of them closer to my heart. I've not trayed my word for any of them."

Gustav argued some time longer, but without luck. He returned to the *Gudvangen* and told Torkjell how things stood. At last he said, "This Olav's always been a sticky man. Now he must mean to run things here only for himself and the ships of Hardanger."

Torkjell said, "You may be right about that. We'll see next summer how far he can do as he means, though." The *Gudvangen* sailed from Stamsund with a full cargo and a Lofoten man called Rolf to see what bargains she might strike in the south.

In the summer also, Olav and Signe settled in a house in Stamsund, a small building, green-painted and well-built, nested among bare rocks that broke some the winds. Late in the year,

Signe bore a daughter and called her Ashild after her mother's mother. The baby was a healthy one and looked likely to live long. Otherwise, Signe kept records at home and stayed mostly out of sight.

Winter in the north is long and dark, though not very cold so near the coast. Olav feared for Signe that she might be too customed to different lands.

One day, Signe seemed more quiet than usual, and Olav marked that she paid little heed to her daughter. He then gave her a box of three throwing knives he had brought from Hardanger.

Signe looked at the weapons. Each gleamed colder than the window ice. She said, "I know little of these things, but they seem fine blades."

"That they are," said Olav, "and better balanced than most."

In the weeks following, Olav taught Signe to throw the knives. She found it a light thing to do and could soon challenge Olav for skill.

The Second Year

Nothing more is told until the next summer, when ships turned to the north. For a time each fjordland ship paid the share Olav had promised from them. Those Stamsunders who had backed the fjordsmen gained more than they could have otherwise.

Then came Torkjell's ship, the *Gudvangen*. Torkjell said he had been paid only a poor price for his cargo; he refused to pay the islanders anything at all. Rolf, the Stamsunder who had sailed with the *Gudvangen* as witness, came on deck and swore that Torkjell spoke only truth. No one believed that, however. They remembered how difficult a man Torkjell had been in the best of times and marked that Rolf never came ashore, even to talk with old friends.

On the night before the *Gudvangen* was to sail, Rolf leaped overboard. He swam his way ashore and ran from the dock. The *Gudvangen*'s watch chased him then and threw rocks after him. One of these hit Rolf on the shoulder and drew blood. But he came free in the end.

Rolf now told his fellow islanders that he had been held on the *Gudvangen* against his will and threatened with death unless he stood behind all that Torkjell said. But the truth was that the *Gudvangen* had made a good deal of money in the south and that the captain hoped to keep it all for himself and his crew.

Rolf's friends came angry at this. They went together to Olav's house to ask him how such a thing could happen. Olav listened to Rolf's story and said, "Never has one Norseman held another as Torkjell has done now, and certainly not just for money." He promised that the *Gudvangen* would pay for the trouble she caused.

Olav told Rolf and his friends to find as many small boats as they could and to set them laying lines across the channel, as many as could be managed. Olav himself went on the pilot who was to guide Torkjell out of harbor and told him to rest in bed.

Torkjell woke early in the morning and saw the sea-spiders weaving their web in the channel. He saw how things must have fallen out and came furious with the watch. He forced three men overboard into the harbor before casting off.

Torkjell stood out to sea without a pilot, going very carefully. He put small boats out to cut through the islanders' ropes. This they did for all the lines but one. This last, however, caught the *Gudvangen*'s rudder and pulled the wheel hard over. The channel is a narrow one in that place; the *Gudvangen* took only a short time to find the rocks.

The crew saw that the ship would either sink as she was or have to recome Stamsund for repair. In any case, there seemed little chance that she would leave the Lofotens under a fjordland captain.

The islanders saw this as well and stayed clear of the Sogn ship, waiting for it to come to their hands without a fight. But

Torkjell was a hard man. He decided to scuttle the ship rather than lose it to other hands. He gave the crew the choice to come with him to the mainland in the lifeboats or to take one of the boats ashore to Stamsund.

Some of the crew were uncertain which course to take. Gustav, Einar's foster brother, said, "This is the work of Olav Whitebrow and his wife Signe. They're the sort who think nothing of turning on their own family to get their way. They won't be kind to people like us." In the end, all the crew went with Torkjell.

The Lofoten boats let Torkjell and his men reach the open sea; they tried to save the *Gudvangen* instead. But Torkjell's old ship settled quickly without him and sank before anything could be taken from her. No more is told of the crew, save that they reached Bodo after some time at sea.

The islanders were of mixed mind about this incident. Some said it showed honor on Olav's part that he had stopped the *Gudvangen* from profiting off her crimes. Others said, however, that the islanders still had nothing to show for their work when all was said and done.

Once again this year, Norse and Scots shared Stamsund's trade between them.

Winter and After

An African warship, the *Urafiki*, came to Lofoten in this winter. The Africans told the islanders that they must choose to trade only with one side or the other by the end of the summer following. Otherwise, said the Africans, one of the rivals might be driven to steal things from the south that no white man should have.

Spring came. Olav had long before promised to travel far to the north and around the North Cape, to see to things there. Now he thought to stay behind to watch the Scots. But Signe said, "Things are slow in the spring. Go as you planned, and I'll look to whatever happens here." In the end Olav gave in.

The days now pass until Signe came to Olav's place to a feast with all the leading men of Stamsund. Signe said little during the meal until someone asked what she thought of the year's competition with the Scots. She answered, "The only thing to fear is that Bruce might challenge us while Olav's away. It's not our custom to turn down a duel, whatever the odds are."

One of the islanders at the feast was called Bjorn Redbeard. He had gained much by trading with the fjordlanders. The next day, he came to see Signe and said, "How have you been born so stupid that you tell the Scots just how to fight against you?"

"It seems I'm bound to be badly thought of," said Signe, "no matter how sociable I try to be."

A messenger from Bruce the Scot also came to Signe's house while Bjorn was still there. He brought a letter that read,

Greetings to my Norse friend,

I have the honor to propose to you this way of ending the dispute that threatens to ruin us both. I challenge you to a contest of arms, the choice of weapon yours, said contest to take place within seven days, and the winner to have sole trading rights in the Lofotens for the next five years.

                                                    Bruce

The messenger did not stay for a reply. Signe showed the letter to Bjorn Redbeard. He said "It's just as I feared. He's lost little time."

Signe now spoke these lines:

> Bruce the laird   of brutes thinks
> I've little   learned my game
> In gab fests   forgets that I
> Know his trade   not he mine

She asked Bjorn to take this reply to Bruce:

Sir:

You leave me no choice but to engage you as you ask. I choose that we use battle knives, to be thrown at targets five meters distant.

Signe

The following day the duelists met at the pier in Stamsund. That is a windswept place with no shelter. It overlooks a bay of rocks. Bruce came with ten Lofoten friends; Signe brought only Ashild and Bjorn. Many other islanders also came, however.

Bruce went first. His friends stuck a plate on the wall of the warehouse before the pier. Bruce's first knife went right into the wall timbers up to the hilt; it took two men to pull it out again. But it missed the plate. His second throw hit the edge of the plate, but did no more. Bruce's third knife, however, struck the plate full and shattered it, though it failed to lodge in the wall behind.

Signe said, "That was fine work. I don't know that I can match it." Bjorn now set a plate against the wall. Signe threw her first knife while Ashild was still on her shoulder; it went through the center of the plate and lodged in the wall.

Bjorn now put up a saucer. Signe put her daughter down, took a mirror from her pocket, and faced away from the warehouse, out over the bay with its seabirds. She threw the second knife over her shoulder; it hit the saucer near one edge and also lodged in the wall.

Bjorn lit a candle and set it on a box in front of the wall. Signe threw her third knife. It cut the burning wick from the candle and left the rest standing, but unlit.

Bruce said, "You've tricked me right and true. But it's still to be seen if the Thing will honor our agreement."

• • •

But many Stamsunders turned from the Scots in the next weeks, even when Bruce offered better terms even than before. Olav found it not difficult to win the day when the Thing met. Bruce left in the fall and was not seen again in Lofoten for a full five years.

Signe and Olav, however, lived on in Stamsund for four years more. They had a further daughter, called Ann, a thin child, but sound of limb and lively. Ashild grew tall and fair. She was a quiet child when with her parents.

At the end of these years, the family recame Hardanger. By this time, Ulf and Britt had a four-year-old son called Gunnar, and a daughter, Grete, two winters old. They were ready now to quit Utne and live on their part of Arnes-stead at Eidfjord. Einar agreed to give them his plot there as well, in turn for the use of Ulf's fishing boat. Olav and Signe took up the house at Utne and lived there from that time on.

Edvard in America

The story now tells of Edvard Ragnhilds-son and how he fared in America after Signe left.

Edvard went west from Wisconsin and came near to Puget Sound with some weeks still left before winter. He stopped in the mountains at a town called Snoqualmie and stayed at the inn there.

A man called Henry lived in those mountains, and came to Snoqualmie off and then. Henry was a bald man of middle height, stout, fifty winters old, and known for fighting. One night Henry played cards with four other men; they had been there some time and come somewhat drunk when Henry said to the man who dealt the cards, "I think you have an extra card in your hand; it's only fair if you put down the deck and turn up your palms."

The dealer said, "I'll not do that just to please you."

"Honest men don't prize their pride so highly."

The dealer grabbed Henry by the shirt; two of the others came after him as well, but the last man backed away. One man hit Henry twice in the face, and another cut the shoulder of his shirt with a knife. But Henry stayed standing because the attackers got each in the other's way.

Everyone at the inn stood to watch the fight, but Edvard came around behind the attackers; he grabbed two of them by the hair and banged their heads together. This distracted the dealer, and Henry soon knocked him down as well.

Henry thanked Edvard and said, "You've made a debtor of me; so now you must come to my house and see if it isn't a better place than the inn."

Henry and Edvard left the inn together and came shortly to Henry's house. It was a low but large building, made of logs, and set in a clearing in the forest.

Edvard could see little of the house at first, aside the light from one window, and in it, the back of a woman's head. Her hair was long and redder than any Edvard could recall. Henry saw Edvard's face and said, "A priest you may be, but my daughter you'd pay to see." Her name was Shiela.

The men came inside. Shiela came to see who had recome home so early in the night. She broke her step for a moment when she saw Edvard, blond, full-bearded, and well-shod. Then she went to help Henry with his wounds.

Edvard stayed ten days with Henry and Shiela. Shiela was then nineteen winters old, slim and light-browed, taller than her father. On some nights, Henry left Edvard with his daughter while he went to the inn.

One night, Henry recame his house earlier than he was customed. He came right to his daughter's room and found Shiela
and Edvard in a single bed. He said to Edvard, "You're making
a priestess of my daughter, as I thought. Many a father would
kill you where you lie."

Shiela replied, "Idle threats are worse than none, Father."

But Henry spoke only to Edvard. "Now you must pay me fairly
and take this daughter off my hands."

Edvard said, "That I cannot, not when my calling lets me
neither to marry nor to father children."

"You can take her whether you marry or not."

"Shiela's a free woman and can go as she likes," said Edvard,
"but I'll pay you nothing in any case."

"Now you're trying to rob me, when I've done no more than
give you roof and bread."

At these words, Shiela rose from the bed, covered in a sheet
and carrying a candle in front of her. She walked up to Henry
and said, "I don't mean to be sold like so much firewood."

"That's more my business than yours," said Henry. He backed
away a step.

Shiela followed him and said, "Do you think yourself the
meaner of the two of us then, Father?" Shiela brought the candle
up near his cheek. Henry said nothing, but caught his daughter's
hand. It went neither forward nor back for some time. At last
Henry twisted her hand and the candle fell to the floor. "That is
not a thing you should have tried," said he. But he left the room
without doing anything more.

Shiela and Edvard talked together for some time. A little before
daybreak, they left the house together and set off for the west.
They soon came to Edvard's rooms at Olalla. There they stayed
together and did not marry.

• • •

Shiela stayed in Olalla with Edvard for the winter, and for eight years after that. At first she was the happiest of women, but after some years, she came lonely living only with Edvard and in the midst of many monks. She thought to have children and mentioned the matter more than once to Edvard.

At last, Edvard said, "I can see my path's a lonely one for you. But we can't have children, as well you knew when you came to me."

"It wasn't all my choice to do that," said Shiela.

But Edvard would say nothing more of the matter, save that Shiela was always free to leave once more, if she must. But Shiela was unwilling to do that either, the more because Edvard was always kind to her otherwise.

In Shiela's eighth year with Edvard, she came pregnant. She told Edvard of this and said, "I wonder what you'll want to do now?"

Edvard answered, "Many women find a way not to be pregnant."

But Shiela said, "I mean to have this child and live with its father as people have always lived. The child's as much yours as mine; and as for marriage, you're my real husband and will be."

Edvard did not know how to answer Shiela for some time. At last he said, "If one of us leaves this place, so must the other. But you ask a lot of me to turn from the God Who's been all my life up to now."

Edvard and Shiela now agreed to go to Norway together. They thought it dangerous to stay in America after breaking an oath to the order. Edvard soon told the fathers of his plan, and of the reason for it. He said, "My sins are great and weigh on me. But this thing I must do; I cannot think God bids me otherwise."

But the eldest father, a man called Christopher, tall, bent, and gray, replied, "That's not a thing for you to say; even we who have lived long will not lightly guess the will of Christ."

The fathers met together the whole of the afternoon. Some among them said that Edvard should be let to go before it could be proved he had broken his oaths. But others thought his a dangerous case and feared that others would follow where one led.

In the end, they agreed that Edvard might leave; but they ordered also that he be branded with the fish, on the right side of the back, facing downward. All the Christians in America know this sign; they shun both it and the back that bears it.

The fathers spared Shiela because she had taken no oath to tray. But both Edvard and Shiela now left Puget Sound by ship. They fared southward to Mexico and crossed that land from west to east. Their child was born on the east coast of Mexico where they waited a ship to Europe. It was a boy, and they called him Lars. The family of three finally fetched Norway seven months after they were sent off from Puget Sound. This was early in November, and almost a full year after Signe and Olav recame Utne from the north.

A Finn Kills Bears

The winter before Edvard and Shiela came to Norway was a hard one. Per Scarmouth showed his age more than in past years. The autumn rainfall sat badly on him; the cold after killed him and many bondsmen also. The winter dealt little death in another respect, however; there were more bears in spring than any in Eidfjord could recall.

A Finn called Jussi came with the spring. He arrived at just the time that Eidfjorders felt most plagued of bears. Jussi was the hardest of men, bald, but still less than thirty winters old. He spoke little and was good at playing the violin. He stayed first in the hut outside the house of Tora the Sniffler.

Youths in the area thought it great fun to laugh at Jussi's bare skull. A few even threw pebbles at his head to see them bounce off, and many teased him to his face. The Finn bore all this in silence.

Jussi heard of the bears roundabout, and also that all the men in the place were afraid to deal with the matter. He said, "I've known many a wolf in Finland harder to handle than any Norse bear."

"Anyone can talk," said Tora, "but the proof's in the kill."

Jussi said no more of the matter then. The next day he took his ax up into the woods above Eidfjord. He did not come back till he had found a bear head to bring with him. He put this trophy to live over the door of the hut he had from Tora, and his deed was soon known over all Eidfjord.

But Tora said, "This isn't much of a test, though it's better than the others have done. Many men in the old days would have thrown back so small a creature. They'd not have needed any great battle-ax to do the work for them either."

Jussi again said nothing, but his mouth had a set look to a Norse eye. He went up the fell once more on the day following, and this time took with him only a knife. He was three days gone now, and came back with the head of another bear, larger than the last. This one he left next to Tora's stove.

Tora said, "This is a fine present, but still only of middling size for a bear. It doesn't look any too bright a beast either. Beside, there were men before who'd not have needed a knife for the deed."

Jussi went off a third time, but now with no weapon at all. Two days passed. Then the whole village could see their Finn stagger down the mountainside. He dragged a whole bear with him, a sleekly fed animal despite the winter. This bear was large enough that it took three ordinary men to move it. Jussi brought the bear to Tora and said, "Save your talk of old men and fill your mouth with bear meat instead."

From this time on, the youths of Eidfjord stepped aside when Jussi passed, even many years later when he was come old and weak.

Ragnhild came to see the bald Finn and said, "There is quite a bit of land in my yard, but I've lost both my houseman and folk to work it. I'll be much in your debt if you will take up a share of it."

Jussi liked this idea better than to stay on in the Sniffler's hut. He moved over to one of the houses at Arnes-stead and set to work farming. He and Ragnhild played music together in the evening from time to time.

Only one thing kept the Finn from being well settled to his new life. He found that there lived a snake beneath his house. He feared the beast might be venomed, and his fear was the greater for that his mother was once bitten by such. This happened when Jussi was quite young and made a great impression on his mind.

The neighbors were no more anxious to be bitten than Jussi was. Tora offered to give him a cat to hunt out the snake. The cat came, but ran off again after a few days and did nothing about its job.

Odd Tors-son was the miller in Eidfjord at the time. He said to Jussi, "That's just what you'd look for from one of Tora's animals. Still, if you like, I can give you a cat of my own. He's never shrunk from game."

Jussi took this second cat home. In the morning there were two mice dead at his door. The second day, Odd's cat brought Jussi a squirrel; a rat and a songbird on the third. But there was no trace of snake.

Finally Ragnhild also gave Jussi a cat. But this animal would not hunt at all, though he never shrank from drinking milk and lying before the fire. Jussi said, "What friends I find here, a vagrant, a killer, and a wastrel, and not one of them does me good." By this time, Jussi could barely sleep at night for thinking

of the snake. It seemed he might have to give up his place, after
all.

Signe came up to Eidfjord to see Ragnhild and Inger. It was
Signe's first visit to Inger after the years in the north, and her
first to Ragnhild after Per's death.

Africa-born Signe found her mother in better spirits than she
had looked for. But she could see that something weighed on
Ragnhild's mind. Signe asked about this after the two women
had been some time together.

Ragnhild explained about Jussi's work with the bears, and also
about his fear of the snake. "I fear," she said, "that I'll soon lose
his help, though he's a better man than I hoped to find."

Signe replied that Jussi sounded a man worth having as friend,
"and there may be some help I can give to him and to you."

Later the same day, Signe caught two mice and set them still
alive in a wooden trap near the snake's haunt. The serpent came
out in the warmth of the day following and found his mice, but
came trapped in the bargain. Signe came and killed the snake
herself. She took the skeleton to Jussi and said, "There's not
much of evil left in this one."

The Finn would not look at the snake. He said, "You've done
me a favor, and my memory's not short. But one thing more you
could do, and that's to take the thing to Tora the Sniffler and tell
her to put it with the bones she's already gotten from me."

Signe now traveled up the fell toward Voringfoss, to the place
where lived her aunt Inger. The two talked only a little as they
often did. Inger had some stray sheep to find and used the chance
to show her niece some the land at a distance from her own, and
as well the hidden trails people had used to come back and forth
to Eidfjord in the bad times when they feared to be followed.
These were now hard to see from disuse.

Beyond that, little happened on this trip of Signe's, or otherwise in the summer.

Knut the Priest

There was in those days a man called Knut. He was the son of a Christian farmer and his wife. The family lived alone above Tyssedal. Their farm was one of those that lie so high that everything passes up and down on ropes. Knut had a single sister named Solveig whom he loved better than any other living thing. The family was quite poor.

Knut grew into a thin man with darkish hair and an unusually long nose. He was strong for his size, and also intelligent. Before many years he found his way down to the fjord so to find his fortune. Knut worked first with fishing boats and came known for his bravery and quick thought. After a few years he shifted to the crew of a trading vessel. In both sorts of ship, he was a good companion, willing to share a drink and spare money for friends. But he recame his own place each winter; he would not be parted from his sister.

Knut was seldom seen in church as a child. Later he shipped twice on the boat belonging to Steingrim the Headstrong. That man worshipped Magni the son of Thor, who fell at Ragnarok. Steingrim seldom looked twice at a man who followed Christ. Knut started to go to shrines and to say verses to Magni, so to be better favored among the crew. But no one marked it that he put much weight on the matter.

It happened one summer that Knut's sister, Solveig Ovretyssedal, saw a single eagle fly overhead to the west. This bird was followed by two ravens. As the ravens came overhead, one of them flew off to the south, but the other stayed and circled for some time. Then it came to ground very near to Solveig and died.

Knut came home for the fall. Soon after that, Solveig fell sick. The illness was a bitter one, with boils on the face and a cough to shake the bracelets. None could remember its like, and no cure offered help.

Solveig then told her brother of her vision from the summer. She said, "It seems most likely that the first bird was Christ our Father, and the others were brother and sister who followed His trail. Is it possible, my brother, that you have done something to go off from the path of right, and so offended the Cross God?"

Knut could look only at the ground. He admitted that he had strayed to another temple, though it had seemed a small matter at the time.

Solveig said, "Then it's certain that this suffering is sent me by Christ. It's so great in any case that I could think of nothing else."

Knut said, "This Jesus is called the God of Mercy. Now's the time to put Him to the test. I promise to pray to no other gods and do every service if He sends you a cure from this disease."

The sister said, "We can only hope that your words haven't come too late. Even a God may have trouble to put things right, though, when I'm as sick as this."

Knut kept up a vigil of prayer in Solveig's room nonetheless, and read long from the Bible. Solveig seemed better in the morning, and still happier the day after that. Knut said, "I can see the power of Christ the Lord. He'll find no followers more devout than we if He keeps His warmth on us and doesn't turn away."

Solveig took a turn downward in the next days, however, and came rather blue in the hands. She stopped taking food, even when she craved it most. Much the time she shivered and could talk little for the chatter of her teeth. She died after four days.

Knut now said, "This Christ is a foul god, to taunt a man with help only to tray him the worse later." He went round the whole farm and broke everything that might have been a cross and burned the Bibles as well. He took this vow: "No man will I let to pray to Christ, no cross to stand, no bell to ring, but ax, fire, and stone will I bring to them instead."

Knut came down the fell to Tyssedal in the spring. He never

recame the family stead. Instead, he sold all he had from fishing and trading, and kept only enough to stay alive. The rest he used to build temples to Magni, the son of Thor, along all the fingers of Hardanger, even on the most outlying farms, there as well.

Knut came a priest of Magni after little more than a year. People came to see him from far places and would be content with no one else. His words sounded most strongly to those who were sick or who had lost a close friend.

Some people called Knut the "wrath of the gods." It happened more than once that his followers burned the houses of Christians, and even of those who spoke their faith in the new gods more softly than Knut was customed to. But all this only made Knut's friends even more devoted to him.

Each year also, Knut and his followers came to the Thing. They tried to outlaw the worship of Christ altogether. But there were never enough votes to carry their law, though their voices were loud.

Knut and Edvard

In the year after Edvard's arrival, all the smiths in Hardanger made themselves into a guild and set a higher price on their work than they had before. There was much grumbling against the Christians for this, and even more after a comet was seen in the winter. Some poor and Christian farmers who had lived south from Odda said this was a sign of the next end of the world. They burned their farms and came down to wander through Hardanger telling their story and begging for food, until they were more than a little hated.

The priests of the new gods said the comet was come from Balder the White, to take all traces of Christ from the land. This word found more favor than that of the farmers from Odda.

Knut Magnis-priest thought all these things boded well for him and his law; he looked never to have a better hope to carry it than in the Thing of the year following, and he set his heart on doing just that. But he could find only scant support from most of the old families as yet; he thought he would need at least one of them to speak strongly on his side, aside from his old friends, if he was to win the day.

Knut heard of Edvard's trial at the hands of the monks in America. He heard also that Ragnhild's son was never known to pray, nor were there any crosses to be seen at his house. Some had it that this was more Shiela's doing than Edvard's. But others said that Edvard let Shiela drive him to what he meant to do in any case.

Knut found his way to Eidfjord late in the winter. He came to Edvard's house with Shiela. Shiela greeted him well and asked him to stop the night. Edvard said that he also was glad to have a guest.

Knut stayed the night. He and Edvard soon fell to talking. Knut described his own dealings with Christ and his hopes for the year's Thing. Then he said, "I've heard that you have reason to feel trayed, you as well."

Edvard agreed that many might think so and told his story. "Still," said he, "I'm not sure how to think about it. Priests don't always act for their gods, as you know."

"It seems to me," said Knut, "that if such can happen here and half a world away as well, this Christ can't be much of a god."

Edvard did not speak to disagree with any of this, but he did not yet promise to back Knut at the Thing either. Knut saw this and said, "The silence of a marked man like you will seem to many to back the church. Why not speak openly of all this at the Thing and let others judge its meaning?"

"That might be the best course. Or perhaps I'll come to see that you're right." Edvard was still unsure how his heart ran, and he did not wish to offend his guest.

•   •   •

Knut thought these words boded well. He spoke also with Shiela and said, "It seems your houseman doesn't yet hate his monks as far as he has the right to."

"So it seems to me," said Shiela. "Still, he's bound to come round in the end. He's a smarter man than most."

Knut left the day after. He was by then sure that Edvard would speak for him, or at the least hold his silence.

Edvard talked with Shiela about Knut's idea that he speak at the Thing against the Christians. Shiela said, "You've not been a priest in all the time since we left America. You don't even say prayers by yourself, so far as I can hear. Why not say in public what you already believe at home?"

"It's true I haven't prayed for a long time. But perhaps that's because I don't feel worthy of the Lord, and not because I hate Him. It's not so easy to forget my early days."

Shiela came close to anger. "You're a first-rate fool if you can't repay these hypocrites and torturers as they deserve."

There came a further visitor to Edvard's house with Shiela early in the spring. This was Gustav Karls-son, who had been Einar's foster son. He was now recome Hardanger as he had promised Einar he would. Gustav was by now a full and paid priest of Christ. He was grown into quite a large man, not tall, but heavy with muscle and fat. He had golden hair and a thick beard, which he used to cover most of his birthmark; his voice filled the largest hall. He was married to a woman named Helga and had two children, twins called Kjell and Enok. Now he thought to get Edvard to help him beat back Knut at the Thing.

Shiela gave Gustav but a cool welcome, and offered neither food nor a place to stay the night. And Edvard took a dislike to his guest almost at once.

Gustav said to Edvard, "I think you know of Knut and his

plans. It's my guess that he'll have a hard time of things ever after if he's beaten now. There's a good chance to make that happen, too, if some new voices will speak against him and bring people to reason. My own word will do some good, of course, but it will be better still if the Thing can hear from some men like you."

Edvard replied, "I have grievances enough against the church not to do the first thing a priest tells me."

"You don't have to say much. Just second what I say."

"We'll have to see how things are at the time," said Edvard. "But I make no promises, even to a man humbler than you."

Gustav left soon after.

Edvard spoke finally with his sister Signe. She said, "I think you're a fool to be a Christian in the first place. Still, it's better to have a folly than nothing at all."

The Thing

Edvard now broods with his thoughts till the time comes for the Thing. Then he rides down to Kinsarvik. Knut is also there, and says to Edvard, "I hope you're ready to speak for my law."

Edvard replies, "I mean to say something on the matter, yes."

Knut says, "Good. Here's what I think is best for you. Say nothing to the earlier laws that come up, so your voice will count for more at the end. When the law comes up, speak only near the end; we can hope that people will have your words in mind when they vote."

Edvard takes this advice in good spirit and says, "I'll be the last to disappoint you."

When Gustav hears of this talk, he says, "It's for the best to lose so vengeful a voice."

• • •

All the Thing now falls out as Knut has planned. Edvard says nothing through the whole time, even when people put forward laws he has some feeling for.

Soon the Thing nears its end, and the time is come to argue Knut's Christian law. Many people stand and give their views and for the most part say no more than they have before. People pay most heed to Gustav Christs-priest because he is new to the Thing. He speaks strongly, and longer than any other, and sits back, well content.

Now Edvard Ragnhilds-son rises. Knut has told his followers to look for a friend in Edvard; many who are unsure how to vote also go silent for him. Ragnhild and her family were highly thought of.

Edvard speaks in this way: "I know many of you think that Christ has hurt you and His followers made you trouble of all kinds. Of you all, I have the greatest complaint—I alone have felt my flesh burn under the iron of His priests, and for no greater a sin than that my wife Shiela was with child. And I was not a heathen to whom no feeling was due, but a full and loyal priest of the God.

"But who can know the will of a god? It was not Christ Who burned my back, but only His priests. It is not Christ Who has hurt you, but only some who claim to be His servants.

"But I think these servants and my priests had God's will wrong. The Christ many of us know would not do such things. The God Who spoke to me was a guide; He led me to all the good things I knew, and spared me from danger in Africa and America. He touched me as He has many others, and left room for no other gods.

"This law will not hurt those who prey on you—they care little for any god and will find it a light thing to change the image on their altars. It will hurt only those who cannot flee from Christ if they would, I among many of you. You can outlaw the priests and punish the smiths if you like, but not in this way."

• • •

Knut sees that many people have listened closely to Edvard's speech; he comes more angry than any has seen him for several years and says, "Every Christian's a liar, but I'll repay this one myself if it takes all my years to do it."

But Gustav Christs-priest has no more liking for Edvard's words; he thinks that Edvard has looked only at him every time he spoke of priests. Gustav says, "This man thinks he can insult whomever he likes. But the time will come when I give that whole family of Ragnhild's something to think about."

Now comes the vote, when all Thingmembers go to one side or the other. The tally shows only a few more in favor of the law than in past years, not enough to win the day. Soon after this, the Thing ends, and everyone rides off from Kinsarvik, each to a different house.

Michael Signes-son

But now, despite Knut's threats, the fjordlands were come on the lordly times, when years passed by three or four at a time, and each more fruitful than the last. Apples and pears weighed on the trees as never since the world's end, and even a low bondsman could live as well as a rich farmer was used to. One could almost think old quarrels dried up under the long summer suns or drowned in the sweet nights of fall.

Only a little is told of Signe in those years. One thing is of a time when Olav Whitebrow was made Lawspeaker at Kinsarvik for the first time. A stranger youth came to Hardanger by ship in the fall of that year; he was a thin lad, brown-haired and still unbearded; he could say but a few words of Norse. Nonetheless, he was able to ask his way to the house of that Signe who was born of Africa.

People guided him to Utne, where he hobbled right up to Signe's house with Olav, knocked on the door. He spoke in English to the woman who answered the door, "If what I hear is right, this house belongs to the one who promised me a bed and a seat of honor in Norway. I wonder if there's anything you can tell me of that?"

It was Signe herself who stood to greet her son. She was surprised to hear English and could not think what to answer for a moment.

Michael spoke again. "I see by your nose that you are truly my mother whom I've missed for many years past. I think you'll not have forgotten this foot of mine that caused such problems before."

Mother and son greeted each other long and well. Signe said, "Tell me how it is that you come now when I looked to see you a year ago or not at all?" For Michael was now seventeen winters old.

Michael said that he had stayed in America to help his father. The two of them had stood back to back through all Stephen's bad times, and had come to see only the best in each other. Michael also brought a letter to Signe from Stephen. This read:

Signe,

I know you found it bitter when you parted from Michael. I hope you find him as promising now as then; I've come to love him well.

Stephen

Signe gave a feast for her eldest child and set him at the head of the table. Olav also gave his stepson a hearty greeting and grudged him nothing.

Michael now stayed the winter at Utne, a quiet lad and helpful. Ann was particularly fond of him, and he taught her how to carve wood. But in the spring, he left Signe's house with Olav and found a place working aboard a ship. He told his mother the reason for this: "You've given me all you promised. But I can't stay here to take the house from under Olav's children. I'll go to get the money I need for my own place instead, and then you can all visit me if you like. Perhaps, though, you'll let me to winter here for a year or two longer."

Signe replied, "There's bound to be a place here for you, whenever you wish it."

Michael went to sea each summer for several years after that. At the last, he had the money to buy a small stead near Ullensvang. There he moved from Utne, but still set out to sea in the summer, as oft as not.

Childplay

During the first year that Michael went to sea, there happened a thing that seemed of little importance at the time.

Ulf Pers-son, Einar's brother, had in turn a son with Britt Jansdatter, as already mentioned. The lad was by now nine winters old, thin and lively. He was his father's greatest joy. In this year, and near to the height of summer, Gunnar went to visit his uncle Einar's farm at Kvanndal.

There is nothing told of this visit till the day that Einar's sons, Helgi and Bjorn, suggested to Gunnar that he come with them to climb in the mountains behind Kvanndal. Helgi was thirteen and a big fellow already; Bjorn was also large for his fourteen winters. Neither was thought a gentle child, however.

The three cousins set out together. All passed well until they came to a place where the path crossed a narrow ledge. Bjorn went across first. Then Gunnar started after him. When he was half the way across, the ledge came loose under him. He fell, and not far before he caught his right foot between two rocks. This trap broke his leg; even so, he had luck with him not to fall farther.

Helgi now stood fast on his side the ledge. Bjorn set out to try to reach his cousin and reach the homeward side. But Helgi could see that this way was dangerous for his brother and called to Bjorn, "Go back to where you were, and I'll go home to tell Father how things are for us."

Bjorn did as he was told, and Helgi wasted no time to reach home. Einar was there, but only two bondsmen were nearby. Einar soon understood what was happened. He brought rope and an ax from the barn and took the two bondsmen up the fell with him. The three followed Helgi to the ledge where Gunnar lay.

The three men found places to fix the ropes. Einar lowered himself to Gunnar. He freed the boy's foot and hooked him to the rope to be hauled up. Then Einar also came up on a rope, but the hillside gave way as he left it. The bondsmen threw a rope to Bjorn. He had little trouble to find his way back across the gap. Once all were on the right side of the ledge, the men felled small trees and laced rope around and over them, so to make a litter to carry Gunnar home. It was slow work but safe to get everyone back down to the farm. Here they came just when dinner was ready.

Gunilla heard the story and said, "You're a silly man, Einar, to carry on in this way, when less important people could have risked their necks just as well. Still, there's this good in it, that no one will call you a coward from now on." She set Gunnar's bone with a splint and bandaged his cuts. But she always blamed Ulf's son for leading her own into danger.

The next day, Einar brought Gunnar across the fjord to see Signe, so he might have a doctor's care. In a few days more, Gunnar came home to Eidfjord. Jussi the Finn visited and said, "It's good to see a lad who's so brave at curing himself." He gave the boy a crutch he had carved from some old wood.

But Ulf said, "Einar's earned whatever he wants from us now, though he was no more than a brother before."

And Britt his wife said, "One can only hope he doesn't ask too high a price."

Gunilla Dies; Einar Grieves

The lordly times lasted several years more. But then came a time less happy. The winters sat deep and white on the land, but the summers were still worse, so wet and filled with rain that even potatoes shriveled in the ground.

Almost every family in Norway suffered from some disease or other in those years, even when they had food enough. Ann Olavs-datter was eleven winters old in the first of the bad years, a cheerful child, thin, and fond of reading. Now her eyes came red and swollen; she could see only in blurs.

Signe stayed with Ann when she could but was gone from her house most of the time; she treated most of the sick near Utne, and not her own daughter only. Signe told Olav that Ann must not come out into the sunlight, nor read or carve wood for the whole of the summer. "Even so," she said, "I fear she'll never see close things again, if she's like most with this illness."

Olav replied, "You know what you speak of; but I know our daughter." He took to reading to Ann every night for the summer. Even when Ann's eyes seemed worst, he would say nothing of them to her save, "Time heals everything, one way and another."

One time, Signe asked Olav to help her patch the roof during an evening. Olav was usually very careful of his house, and especially of leaks in the roof. But now, he hardly heard Signe's words and replied, "I'm doing the more important thing already."

In the autumn, Ann recovered and could see as well as anyone. Olav never spoke of the matter more; and Signe said, "It seems that two doctors are better than one."

Even in the beggar times, however, there were some who thought to live as well as ever. It is said of Gunilla Auduns-datter that she died of a piece of meat she caught in her throat in the third of these years. Whatever is the truth of that, many believed it. Signe said, "It's too true not to be so."

Gunilla had come sharp of tongue in her last years, and less openhanded than before. There were not many tears shed at her funeral; even Einar looked to bear the loss well. But later, he took to his room for weeks at a time. Helgi and Bjorn were now grown into young men, short of patience and quick to take offense. They thought Einar's grief had no point and tried to bring him back to good cheer. But their efforts came to nothing.

Toward midwinter, Bjorn went to Halmar Vidals-priest, who lived nearby. Halmar was a laughing man, and fond of living as well as the times allowed. He was counted the third most kindly priest in Hardanger and was known for sleeping only one night in two; on the other he walked outdoors, even in the most bitter of weather. Bjorn said to him, "My father's never had much use for the gods before. Still he's so far downcast now that nothing we do has any effect, and he's made himself a great nuisance to us. We hoped for you to come and help us in some way."

Halmar said, "I'll be happy to come, and within the week. In this case, my duty leads me where I'd like to go in any case, since Einar Pers-son is a famous man." The priest came to Kvanndal not many days later and stayed for three days.

Halmar told Einar that the gods had no use for men who pined the seasons past. Gunilla's death was the saddest of things, but still, a man's life had more to it than his wife only. Gunilla's fate was no fault of Einar's, in any event, though he might well be blamed for the way he carried himself now.

Einar said nothing to all this, no more on the third day than on the first, but turned his head to face the wall. Halmar came to leave; he said to Einar's sons, "I'm sorry at the turn things have taken, that all my talk does no more good than ants against the sea. Still, there's not much point to my staying longer when others can use me better." The sons thanked him for his efforts and saw him off once more.

* * *

Einar got no better after that, but stayed in bed even more. He refused to get up except when the sun shone, and the days were then very short. Helgi now said to Bjorn, "Things are going from bad to worse. Halmar's not the only priest in Hardanger, nor even the strongest, if what people say is true. We've little to lose by asking Knut Magnis-priest to come to treat our father."

Bjorn agreed to this and fetched Knut to Kvanndal. That man came soon after the year turned.

Knut talked some time with Einar. Then he recame the sons and said, "Your father's in the grip of some evil thing. I can try to break its hold if you like, but it may hurt him some on the way."

Helgi answered, "It's no good thing to wish harm on one's father, but it's still less good for him to stay as he is, good for nothing."

Knut now clad himself in a long black cape. He went into Einar's room and burned some plants, till the room filled with smoke. He doused all light in the room, save a single torch behind where he stood. All this time, Einar lay with his face to the wall and said nothing.

At last Knut spoke: "Einar, listen now to the voice from the gods, from Vidar and Vali, Odins-sons; from Magni, the son of Thor, with the hammer of fire; and from the shade of Balder, most pure."

Einar gave no sign, so Knut stuck him with a pin. Einar jumped as he lay, and turned to face the priest.

Knut said, "Your wife is dead, and you killed her. Do you think it enough to lie here whimpering for months on end?"

Einar said, "I never killed her."

"You wanted her dead, though. For years you've dreamed yourself free of her and having a life with other women—and not only in your sleep."

Einar said nothing; Knut went on, "You, Einar Pers-son, you gave Gunilla the meat that killed her. You wanted her dead and you killed her. It's as great a deed as you've ever done, though your paltry soul can't stand by it now."

Einar still said nothing, and turned his back once more. He soon fell nearly to sleep, but Knut poked him with another pin and said, "Killers can't sleep as lightly as you'd like."

"I'm no murderer," said Steadholder Einar.

"Your heart's more open to me than it is to you," answered Knut, "though that's common enough."

"What kind of man are you to come and insult a grieving man?" asked Einar. "I'm no common man, either, after a life like mine."

"Anyone who fears his own god is vulgar—though hardly alone."

"I have no god."

"Ah. But you do. Only the god in you could have led you to kill. You'd just like to fool yourself and your fate afterward."

Einar now tired of the argument and turned away. The day went dark with evening, and smoke made the room murkier even than before.

Knut lit a small bomb and set it off. Einar jumped again. Knut said, "Now I'll tell you of the women you'd like to sleep with." He described first Einar's mother Ingeborg.

When Einar saw who this was, he said, "Shut your mouth, you toad of a priest. Who are you to speak, you who loved his sister for all the world to see?" Einar climbed from his bed and tried to grab Knut. But the light was so bad that Einar could not tell what was Knut and what cloak. He ran his head into the wall through the cloak and fell to the floor. The blow knocked the torch from the wall as well.

Knut caught Einar with a pin, while the steadholder still groped about on his knees. Einar flung his arms in the hope to hit the priest; he stood for a short time, and then fell over his own bed and lay still.

Knut picked up the torch, stepped on the sparks it left behind, and put it back on the wall. Then he said, "This woman you wanted most is dead. Yet still you killed your wife to get her."

"No."

"Not only for that, you mean." Knut described some of the women who lived near Kvanndal, one after the other. At the last, he mentioned Tordis, a bondswoman who was said to have the neatest house in Hardanger. "Where would it be best to have her?" he asked. "In the barn, perhaps, or on a summer day in the pig wallow?" Einar smiled at this last.

Knut stabbed him once more with a pin. "To Hel and Niflheim with you. You think you have only to smile once or twice to be at peace. Let's talk of the men in your mind."

"You can't read my thoughts," said the steadholder. But his voice was not strong.

"There's nothing easier, when half the world can guess them." Knut described Petter Gorms-son. Einar groaned and tried to stand. But he fell back flat on his bed instead and into a deep sleep.

Knut left him then and was careful to block the door so that Einar could not get out. Knut recame the room off and then through the night, and woke his charge with a pin or a bomb.

The priest's second day in Kvanndal dawned with a fog that lifted and fell as it pleased. Knut went on with his work much as on the day before. But on this day, Einar agreed with all the priest had to say; the steadholder spent most the time kneeling and crying.

The third day was the same. Einar came more quiet and listened with care as Knut told him how to pray to Magni Thors-son.

The next morning there was a light snow. Knut left Kvanndal. Einar was well enough in a few days that he would talk to his sons, and even with people who came to see him.

In the spring, Einar moved everything out from the room that had been his with Gunilla and had it burned. He set a small statue of Magni at one end of the room, and, over the statue, a hammer, a belt, and a glove. Below was an altar. Einar bought as many gold cloths as he could find to put on the walls around the room, and replaced the wood floor with one of stone. This was said to be the richest temple to Magni at that time, though not the warmest.

Einar was fully come to his senses by this time. He made over his whole house and started once more to give feasts for his neighbors when he could. Now, however, he never failed to ask Knut to join the meal, and he sat the priest at the high table. Einar always called Knut "my saver," and people marked it that this seemed not to upset the priest very far.

Ulf came to Kvanndal after the Thing that summer and saw how his brother fared. He said to his nephew Helgi, "Your idea to use a priest has certainly borne a good deal of fruit. Still, some might find it bitter to the taste."

Helgi replied, "Something's better than nothing."

And Bjorn said, "He's our father, and we mean to do what we can for him, even when others can't be bothered."

All Hardanger soon heard of the miracle at Kvanndal. Many thought that Knut was shown to be among the greatest of priests for his success in so difficult a case. But Halmar said, "Knut kills people to cure them."

Ashild Marries

The skies came clear in the third spring after Gunilla's death, and people looked for better times. In the event, though, the summer was only a little drier than the one before.

Ashild and Ann, Olav's daughters, were living still at home in Utne. Ashild was now eighteen winters old, fair, tall as her father, and the most sought of women. She also cared more for furniture than for wayfaring, and this habit seldom failed to annoy her mother. One time, Signe said, "Who am I to have birthed a stay-in-the-bed flower?" But Ashild was set in her ways.

Ann was two years younger than her sister, dark-eyed and brown-haired. She seemed to some a bit scrawny. Ann was by now very good at carving wood, especially into long animal shapes. Her work was already better than that of her half-brother, Michael Signes-son. Ann was also good at drawing, but she was not nearly so neat as her sister Ashild.

Michael Signes-son lived still at Ullensvang during the winters, and sailed in summer.

In this summer, Ashild Olavs-datter fell in love with a lad called Villem Jens-son, who came from Na, not far from Utne. The two of them decided to marry in the winter following, despite it that they were both so young. Ashild told all this to Signe.

But the mother seemed cool to the idea and asked, "Are you full sure that this is your wish?" Ashild did not answer at once; Signe said, "I think you'd do better to see more of the world and its people before you tie yourself to one place and one man."

Ashild now replied, "I told Villem we must look for you to stand against us. You've never tried to understand me—or much of anyone else, for that matter. In any case, I know my own mind as well as you do yours."

"Perhaps so," said Signe. "Villem's a nice enough sort, though I've never noticed that he thinks very far ahead."

Ashild's face went a little red at this. She said, "He doesn't lie awake at night to plan out the least move in some game or other. But then, he does know something of love."

Signe now spoke with Olav and said, "I think Ashild's a fool in this, and a young one at that."

Olav replied, "How old would you have her be? At any rate, she's your daughter and mine, and not about to be bullied, even in a good cause. We ought to stand by her."

"I meant to do nothing else," said Signe. "But how can I like it to see my daughter waste her life so quickly?"

"Perhaps we must trust her not to do that, however things seem just now."

Signe said no more then or later. But she was quiet and un-smiling throughout the summer and into the fall; she took to wandering on her own through the mountain forest over Utne.

At last, Ann said to Olav, "We must do something to change the way that Mother thinks about things."

Olav replied, "Yes, but I'm not the one to do it. She knows me too well and sees through me in everything." He thought a moment and said, "I do have some hardwood from Africa. Per-haps there's something you could do with that."

He took Ann to the barn where he had kept the planks of wood for some years. Ann looked at them and said, "There may be something in them, I think."

Ashild and Villem gifted themselves in the winter. Signe and Olav joined the wedding; they came a day ahead of Ann and Michael. At the end of the wedding day, Ashild thanked her mother and said, "We've never had much in common, you and I, for all that we're mother and daughter. But perhaps now we can see each other in the eye more fairly."

"Perhaps," said Signe, and kissed her daughter and smiled. "You've had all I could give you. Now it's up to you to find a use for it."

But Signe did not smile later in the evening when Ashild and Villem had left, nor in the morning when she and Olav set out for home.

Signe and Olav came to Utne along with Ann. It happened that throughout the fall, Ann had worked secretly on a new bed for her parents, carved from the wood Olav had shown her. She had finished it just at Yule. When Olav and Signe went ahead to the wedding before Ann, she set the bed up in her parents' room.

Now Signe and Olav came home to their new bed. The carving on it was the most thoughtful Ann had done up to then; the posts were capped each with a lion's head, and the sideboards decorated with dragons. Signe looked at it a full minute.

Then Ann asked, "Do you like it?"

"It is beautiful," said Signe Ragnhilds-datter, "and well you know it." Both she and Ann laughed.

The winter passed more happily after that. Olav seemed more than a little sad when the time came for him to travel north for the spring.

Death of a Catholic

In the days before Ragnarok, when all the gods slept save only Christ on His cross, many sorts of Christians walked among us, and not only the Lutherans of today. There were some who were known for honoring a man called the Pope, who lived in a southland city of seven hills called Rome. The Pope's people called themselves Catholics, though other people gave them different names.

For many years before the war, no one cared much that some worshipped the Pope while others followed Luther, and many never thought of the gods at all. But in after times, people looked to blame each the other for the smallest things; then the Lutherans would no longer pray for the Catholics and refused to let them share in any service.

There were never many Catholics in Hardanger, and even fewer with each year. It was difficult to be a Christian even with friends to help. Nonetheless, there was one man to stay faithful to the Pope, even up to the time of this saying. His name was Harald, and his mother Sigrid had been a Catholic in her time also, and a strong-willed woman. In all the years, Harald had not once gone to the Lutherans' church; for most of the time, he had no place at all to pray.

By now, Harald was an old man, many years white of both hair and beard. He lived alone with his wife Louisa in a small place near Ulvik. Their land was thought poor because it often flooded.

It happened late in the spring that one of Harald's legs swelled up and that he heard the voices of angels in his sleep. At this, he thought himself a dying man and brooded how best to meet his God. One day, just after the Thing, he said to Louisa, "It seems to me that I've been no more stubborn than these Lutherans. But it's still a bad bargain to go to God unblessed, and still worse to be buried in the heathen way. I want you to go to the priests and ask them to see me before I die. They can say whatever verses they like, even if they're not the Pope's."

Louisa agreed to do this. She went to the churches near Ulvik. But at each place the priest refused to come, but said that a lifetime of bad ways wouldn't wash out in an hour's blessing.

At last Louisa came across the fjord to Brimnes to see Gustav Christs-priest, the foster son of Einar. Gustav was still a heavy man, and it was said he hated as many people as he loved, whatever Christ might say of the matter.

Louisa told Gustav her errand. The priest answered her, "There's nothing I can do to help you myself, because I have many who worship at this church, and who'd not like it if I helped a Catholic. But this you might do—go to Edvard Ragnhilds-son in Eidfjord. He once was a priest, and he's got no flock to lose."

Louisa thanked Gustav for his help and left. Gustav, however, mentioned the matter to his two sons, Kjell and Enok, and also to various other people, among them Sigurd Kristins-son of Ulvik. Sigurd was a friend of Knut Magnis-priest, and an important man in upper Hardanger. Gustav told him of Louisa's visit and said, "I hope Edvard can help this man; it's sad when anyone goes to death unblessed."

* * *

Louisa came home with Gustav's idea. Harald heard her out and said, "I've heard that there's a grudge between this Gustav and Edvard. Perhaps he means to use us to settle the account."

"That may well be so," replied Louisa. "Still, you've no choice but to ask Edvard if you want any blessing at all."

"It will take a night's thought," said Harald.

Harald slept through the night. It seemed to him that the angels flew lower over him than before, so near, in fact, that he could feel the wing feathers on his face, and feared to wake. But then he also heard the nearest angel say, "Noble is the man who suffers on the Lord's path."

In the morning, Harald told his dream to Louisa and said, "Now you must go to Edvard, the son of Ragnhild, and tell him of my dying and my dream. But say also this, that some dreams are false, and that we have no wish to shame him into something unwise."

Louisa took this message to Edvard's house with Shiela in Eidfjord. She laid the whole matter before Edvard and said, "We're resolved to rely on your judgment of the matter. But one thing I fear, that you must make your mind quickly, or else death will make it for you."

Edvard gave no answer at once, but went to talk with Shiela. She was working among the cabbages. Edvard told her of Louisa's errand. Shiela said, "Even you must know that your enemies look for just this sort of thing to hold against you."

"That's true enough," said Edvard. "But life is not so great a gift that I can grudge it to God when He asks it."

Shiela looked at her cabbages for a moment and then said, "The weak often see God's hand in everything that passes. You risk leaving me a widow and our children orphans if you do this."

Edvard answered, "I've failed the Lord too often before; I can't grudge Him so simple a thing."

"Then do as you will," said Shiela. "We can hope for the best,

though this Christ of yours has brought nothing but bad for me."
She turned back to the garden and said nothing more.

Edvard soon left Eidfjord in company with Louisa. They
sailed down the fjord and back up to Ulvik. The water was
very smooth and the mountains bright in the sunlight. They
came to Harald's house late in the day; for the last part of the
journey, they marked a sail on the same course as theirs, but
a little behind.

By this time, Harald was a weak man. Edvard read to him the
Catholic verses for holy days. Harald said, "You have let me die
better content than I hoped to be."

But he did not die straightaway. Louisa gave Edvard dinner
and put him to sleep near the fire.

Early in the morning, Louisa waked her guest. She said, "I
hear a thief outside." But Edvard could find no one near the
house.

Harald called for Edvard when the morning was full come.
He said, "Time is heavy on me; I fear not to live out the hour."
The old man had trouble to breathe, and his pulse came only in
bursts. He could feel nothing over one side of his body.

Edvard said the man's final rites. This morning, Harald was
as good as his words; he died without speaking again. Louisa
stayed with her husband some time longer and wept.

After a time, Edvard asked, "Have you friends roundabout,
who might help us to bury Harald?"

She replied, "We have only two friends, and both are nearly
as old as I. Still, they'll lend a hand."

Edvard, Louisa, and the two friends buried Harald in the evening. Edvard spoke a full grave service over the fallen Catholic.

Edvard's Trial

On the morning following, and quite early, ten men came to Harald's old house with Louisa. They were all followers of Knut Magnis-priest, and friends of Sigurd Kristins-son. Sigurd himself was at their head.

Edvard came from the house to meet them. The men took him by both arms and carried him off to boats they had waiting in the fjord, not far off. Sigurd took Edvard to Kinsarvik, where they came late in the day.

Knut was one of the seven elder priests for the year. He was at Kinsarvik when Sigurd arrived. Sigurd came at once to Knut's house and told him what had happened and what could be said against Edvard.

"I've waited a long time for Edvard to make his mistake," said Knut. "I think he'll not make another."

Knut sent some of Sigurd's men to fetch the other elder priests and set the rest to stop anyone from sailing out over the fjord to carry the alarm to Edvard's sister Signe, or to his other friends. He kept as well one man to stand guard over Edvard for the trial to come. This was Goran the Swede; Goran was a pious and trustworthy man, but he was not generally thought very clever.

The elder priests gathered at the temple that stands in the old sheep meadow over Kinsarvik. It was early in the evening. Three of the elder priests were friends of Knut's; they most often went along with whatever he said. Another was Halmar Vidals-priest; but his voice seldom carried the day.

There could be no doubt that Edvard had said Christian verses in the open air on the day before when he helped to bury Harald the Catholic. Several of Sigurd's men had watched him from hiding; Edvard himself did not deny it. Knut said that Edvard must die for his crime.

The other priests feared that Knut was carried away by his old grudge, however. They would rather wait for the Council to meet and say judgment over Edvard. But they were not willing to do this unless Edvard swore that his verses had been false and of no standing. They wanted as well his promise to say no more verses till the Council met.

Edvard agreed to say no further service. But he would not foreswear the verses he had given Harald. He said, "I will not give up something that meant everything to that man." Edvard would say no more than that, though he was asked to several times.

In the end the elder priests came more cross at Edvard than they were at Knut. They did not think they should stand guard over Edvard's life when he cared so little for it himself. They agreed at last that Edvard should be stoned to death if he would not relent by morning. But Edvard stayed steadfast.

Early on the next morning, Sigurd and his men left the tents they had pitched near the water and brought Edvard to a place just south from the town. This place is ever after called Edvard's Hollow. It is wrapped on three sides by rock. The elder priests came also, all except Halmar; he stayed at home in his bed. About thirty townspeople followed behind, for the most part fishermen who were at home; they had never been fond of Christians.

Knut Magnis-priest stepped forward and said, "Edvard Ragnhilds-son, I greet you. By the power given me by the law and by the twin staffs of Vali and Vidal, I tell you that you are to die. Our gods are more merciful than yours, though, even in treating with an enemy. You may take up the sword against any single man here and so earn a warrior's death, despite the rest of your life."

Edvard said, "You're about to have blood on all your hands. There's no reason to share it with me."

Knut said, "You have the right to die in disgrace, naturally." He spoke to the crowd, "The man before us is to give his blood that the children of the Aesir and of the Vanir may not forsake this land, nor give it back to Christ the Meek. Let him who has lived longest throw the first stone."

Fredrik Tremble-tongue took a rock and threw it at Edvard. He missed the mark, and the stone hit on the cliff behind Edvard with a small sound. Edvard said, "May God forgive the rest of you as easily."

These words angered the crowd. They rushed headlong at Edvard and threw rocks as they went. Edvard soon fell and died. He was largely covered with rocks in a few minutes.

The townspeople went away soon after. Sigurd's men also left, all but Goran the Swede, to recome their tents. But Goran stayed behind for some time, even after Knut and the other priests were gone. He stood and looked at the body.

Signe Buries Her Brother

By mid-morning, Signe heard of Edvard's fate on her farm with Olav at Utne. She came across the fjord and went first to see Edvard's body. But she did no more than touch the corpse; Goran watched her in silence.

Signe now went to the two Christian churches near Kinsarvik. She met Anders Christ-priest at the first and said, "My brother was of your faith. He lies dead, as you know, and for his Christian deeds. He must be buried in the Christian manner and with the Christian words. I wonder what you can do to help."

Anders answered, "Your whole family's arrogant when you ask such a thing of me. Edvard died for trying to save a poper from hell. That's a pointless errand, and he got no more than he could have guessed. Let him lie for his folly."

Hakon the Longwind was priest of the second church. He said, "I always had love for your brother as one man of the cross must for another. But God bids us be meek before the law; I'd only offend two swords if I did as you ask."

Signe traveled up to Brimnes next and stopped at the church of Gustav Christs-priest. She asked the man also if he would come to say the graving rites for Edvard. She finished by saying, "You of all people should do this, you who did so much to bring his death about."

"I don't know what you mean," said Gustav, "but it sounds none too friendly, in any case. As for Edvard, he met a martyr's death; it's a glorious fate to earn. But you haven't the right to ask others to seek it as well."

Signe said, "I've long thought of Christians what now I know. I won't ask this of you again—Edvard's better off not to be buried by cowards."

Signe rode off up the fjord once more. She reached Eidfjord and Edvard's house with Shiela late in the afternoon. Shiela greeted her sister-in-law: "Hail and say what tidings come so fleeting."

"No more than you already know—or can guess quickly enough."

"Then it would have done as well to wait," said Shiela.

Signe gave no sign that she heard these words but said, "I've come to ask you to help me to give Edvard a Christian grave."

"I loved the best of your brother," said Shiela. "But his Christ was crueler to me than my father."

"Edvard was a Christian and your husband, however you like to think about it."

"He chose that path without thought for me or for our children. He can finish it on his own, too."

"Yet he stayed by you through many bad times. Now his body lies broken and unburied. That can't seem right to the lover of any God—or of none."

"I mean to honor Edvard in my own way. You won't shame me into anything else."

Signe said, "It's a craven crow that clings to its pride."

Signe came home late in the evening. On the day following she asked Ann to dig a grave in the yard near the house. In the evening she went back to Kinsarvik to the place where Edvard lay. It was near to dark when she began to clear the stones off Edvard's body. The night came dark and misty as she worked. After a time, Signe saw the light of a torch coming to meet her. It was Goran the Swede. He spoke first, "Who is it that dares bother this place?"

"I am my brother's sister," said Signe, "come here to honor his life over the mindless stones."

"Then," replied the Swede, "the same fate will fall you that felled him."

"Not from you, at any rate." Signe threw a rock at Goran. It hit him full on the forehead, but not very heavily. "Good fortune for you, Goran, that you're not worth the trouble of a knife."

Goran went off and came to the house of Knut Magnis-priest. Knut met him and saw that his forehead was bloody. Goran told him what had happened with Signe, and asked what Knut thought he might do now.

Knut replied, "Go follow Signe and watch all that she does, so that you can swear to it later. I think she must mean to take the body back to Utne, since she won't find it easy to make a grave here. I'll be sure that you have a way to follow her."

Goran left Knut's house; Knut went to wake Sigurd and his men from their tents. They had several boats still at Kinsarvik and could follow Signe, if need came.

Goran now met Halmar Vidals-priest on the road. The priest was out walking as he was customed to do. He took Goran to his house and bandaged his forehead. Goran explained all that he meant to do. Halmar said, "You'd do much better to let her do things in her own way and pay no heed."

Goran said he could not do that, since all Sigurd's men were to go with him. "Then I'd best go myself," said Halmar, "since those are dangerous men to send all together."

• • •

By this time, Signe had finished uncovering Edvard's body. Signe's hair was still brown in this year, and her face only slightly wrinkled, with a nose long and straight; her fingers were somewhat crooked from many years of work; she liked to crack the knuckles to scare children when they were unsettled. She was still not a heavy woman, and her ankles unusually thin, so that people wondered how she carried anything for long. Now she was dressed all in white, with a purple cord to knot the dress around her waist and a purple scarf over her hair. She was barefoot as well.

Signe took Edvard's body onto her shoulder and started to carry it off. The way to the fjord was downhill, but the burden still more than she was used to. Goran and Halmar met her halfway and followed her down to the shore.

Signe came to her boat. Several more men came up to her, and with torches. The torches glowed yellow in the fog and passed the light from one face to the next. Signe said nothing, but put the corpse into the boat.

Halmar Vidals-priest now spoke: "I see your silver face is bravely set, Signe. We wish it no harm."

Signe turned from her boat and said, "Leave me to bury what's mine, then."

"That we cannot. The body you carry off belongs neither to you nor to the ground. It's cursed of the gods and must lie unmarked."

"So you say," said Signe. "But you'll need more help than you have here to stop me."

Some of Sigurd's men said that they should take Signe up to the temple as they had her brother before her. But Halmar told them, "Signe's lived here too long; she can't be judged by priests."

Signe pushed her boat into the fjord and hoisted her sail. Sigurd's men went to the village docks nearby and set out after her. Some among them were skilled sailors; they had little trouble to catch Signe before she reached Utne.

Signe berthed her boat. She lifted Edvard's body and carried it up to her own stead. The men with torches followed her until she reached her own yard. Here Signe stopped and said, "I can't stay you from following me further. But now we are on land that none of you can claim; you come against the will of those who can."

Two of Sigurd's men set fire to a fence rail to show their answer.

Signe went on and soon came to the open grave. She put Edvard to rest beside it and called to Ann, who still waited nearby. Signe said, "It's no crime to dig a hole in the ground, even with hands as skilled as yours. What I'm about to do is not so safe. Be off; if the worst happens, you must remember me and carry my memory to others."

Ann knew her mother's mind and left.

Signe spoke once more to the men with torches: "You've no need of fire. I'll do nothing till daylight." The sky was already gray at this time. But the men kept their torches as they were.

Halmar stepped up some time later and said, "We can't stop your plans. But what you mean to do will put us in a bad place. When you bury an outlaw, you stand to face the crimes he died for. We'll have to speak against you, if it comes to that. I for one will find no joy in that."

"If you don't like to know what I do, you have only to walk away."

"It's the fact we fear, not the knowledge," said Halmar.

Signe said nothing more. She sat silent on a stone to wait for full daylight.

The sun rose and gave all the land to loom pale through the fog. Signe took up her brother's body for a last time and put it into the grave. She spoke these words: "Let morning light show, no trolls grace the grave roads of this man; may his soul find its way safe to Christ at last."

She spoke more softly then and said the Christian death service.

Sigurd's men closed to hear all that she said. Their torches were of little use in the daylight.

Finally, Signe put the Bible Ann had left into Edvard's arms as he lay. She took up a shovel and filled the grave with dirt.

Signe's Trial

Knut Magnis-priest went to Halmar a few days later and said, "I hear that Singe has prayed for her brother and buried him at Utne."

"That may be so."

"And that you were among those who watched her."

"The sun shone badly that morning, and the hearing was none too good in the fog, either."

"You're too soft a man for your place in things here," said Knut.

"There's no profit in it to fight such a woman."

"That you must do, though. Or else, people will know they can ignore the gods as they like."

"Others saw what I did. Any of them can lay the suit, if he likes; I'll do my duty to speak the truth I saw."

"No," said Knut. "You must do it. People trust you further than a man like Goran. It won't hurt you to show you're stout of heart, for the time the temples meet, either."

Halmar called at Signe's. He said, "What I feared is now come about. Knut wants me to charge you with sacrilege for burying Edvard. I might get off without, if you forsake your deed and pay an altar price to the new gods."

But Signe said, "I've no use of gods, new or old. I'll not step back from my brother now, either."

"Then I must charge you for sacrilege here and now, with the suit to face a judge at the fall Council."

"I'll make ready, if you must have it so."

•   •   •

Time now passes until the Council comes to sit. Signe sailed
to it, and most of her friends and close family with her. But Olav
was still in the north, and Ragnhild by now so old that she could
not leave Eidfjord. The priests of the new gods were there as
well, with many hangers-on. Einar came; Ulf was away at sea.

Only forty people stand as judge in the Council. At Signe's
trial many more than that came to watch. The Lawspeaker for
the year was Nils Nedrelofthus.

Halmar Vidals-priest spoke against Signe. He said she had
buried her brother despite his crimes, and that this was sacrilege
according to law and custom. He called witness to his charge.
At the last he said, "Only fear of the gods makes us honor the
other laws over the whim of this person or that; Signe has broken
the highest of the laws."

Signe now rose and said, "I deny nothing that's been said, nor
give any apology. Halmar thinks I've broken the highest of laws,
but he does not say that it was my brother who lay dead, from
stupid blows and a foolish law; he says no more of how we shall
have a strong land when we are content to leave our brothers to
rot.

"As for the gods he speaks of, I have no fear of them, so long
as they strike their own blows.

"Others will have to say who had the right of this case when
they speak of it in later times. I ask no mercy from you, but only
my due—that you blame the law and not me."

Lawspeaker Nils said to the judge, "You forty of the judges
must say your thoughts on this matter. There is no doubt that
Signe Ragnhilds-datter has broken our known law. You may feel
she has the right of the matter, even so. In that case, you may
free her and say the law is wrong. The Thing itself has seldom
said such a thing; a judge has never said so on its own. But the
choice is yours."

The judge divided. Three and twenty walked to the right and

judged Signe guilty. Seventeen went to the left.

The Thingholder counted the sides and said, "The judge finds that guilt lies with Signe Ragnhilds-datter for sacrilege."

Lawspeaker Nils asked Halmar to say what punishment he thought fit.

Halmar thanked the judge for their verdict. He pleaded for mercy in the sentence against Signe; he said a fine should be enough for a woman whom the fates had treated unkindly already. "She acted only for her brother's sake, and in the hardest of circumstance. She's not likely to repeat herself."

But Halmar's was not the only voice. Gustav Christs-priest spoke next: "Christ bids us forgive our enemies, but there must be limits even to His mercy. This woman has defied the children of Odin and Thor; she's stood against Christ also. She spoke our graving rites though she's no priest. She spoke them for a man who gave comfort to a poper. The woman can only hate all the gods. To fine her—that's to ask an ax to be gentle. Only if we cast her out from Hardanger will any god be at peace."

Others spoke as well, for one side or the other. Only two sentences were mentioned, fines and outlawry.

Signe spoke last. She said, "You know already what I think fair, that you offer me praise instead of blame. I don't know how you will speak; however it is, I'll do as I must."

The three and twenty now divided in turn. Thirteen wanted to send Signe into outlawry for three years. The rest favored a fine.

The Thingholder said, "Signe Ragnhilds-datter, I greet you. You are to be counted no part of our land for three years' time. You are to be gone from Hardanger before the next spring. Or else a jury may carry the sentence to you."

Signe came home from Kinsarvik and stayed there through the early fall. One day, she and Ann visited Michael. It was already evening when they came home over the fjord. Signe said to Ann, "How fine the air seems tonight, finer than I've ever thought it, and the sheep bells on the hill. I think I won't leave Norway, whatever happens."

Signe Visits Inger

Signe stayed at Utne two weeks more and then traveled up to Ingers-stead. She said to her aunt, "I've come to a hard pass; I fear it's meant to be the end of me." She explained all that had fallen with Edvard and at her own trial. "Now I need shelter from the winter. I won't leave this land; but I could well drag all my family down with me if I stay at Utne."

Inger asked Signe what made her think that.

Signe replied, "I've had a dream. I could see myself in it, standing in the middle of a field. There seemed to be friends about, though whether people or beasts, I could not rightly see; there was a fog over everything. Across the field came some blind men. The plants smoldered where they stepped; yellow smoke mixed with the fog. There was no sound. They could not sense me, but somehow came near after a time. I reached out and touched some of them; those fell back. But the others closed around me. In the end they trampled me down, blind though they were. My dying hand caught one of them by the wrist or the ankle, I'm not sure. The rest went through the fields and killed everything. Whatever they touched burned; or else it grew a yellow green mold that ate away at it. Everything was soon laid waste in one way or the other. One person escaped their blind eyes and fled. But it seemed that this one also was to fall before them, later if not sooner."

Inger had always made her own liquor. Now she gave some to Signe and said, "In this case, you must make your home here while home there is to make. The sleep tidings are clear enough; an old woman could find a worse fate than to stand by you in this fog of yours. Maybe we can take some payment from them on the way."

The two of them agreed that Signe would stay the winter. They made an extra bed of straw and did what else was needed to make the hut a house for two.

There were still two weeks before the first full freeze and snow. Signe made ready the things she could for the attack she expected in the spring. There is but one main track up to Ingersstead. Signe now went over it with a new eye. In one place, the road goes over a river on a wooden bridge. Signe prized up the planks covering the bridge so they could be moved more easily later.

At another place, the road goes through a tunnel in the mountain. Signe found a place where the roof of the tunnel was coming loose. She pulled down some of the rocks, and left the rest so they would fall when first disturbed. With all this work in hand, she recame Inger's hut. The nights began to be quite cold.

Life in the fells went on quietly for some weeks. The kinswomen made fast for the winter and were happy to play cards together. Inger also whittled.

The first big snow of the winter came. Signe and Inger could see that it had snowed lower down as well. Signe said, "Now I must go to the fjordlands a last time." She wanted to say farewell to her family and bring back some things she needed for the spring.

Inger replied, "Take my sledge, in that case, and as well my horse. Yours is not used to heavy work."

"I hoped to borrow the sledge," said Signe. "There will be much to carry. But Thorsvenn should stay here, since I'm taking too much from you already."

"Why should I grudge you my horse, you who will have my life? What is right is that you take everything that will make better the end of this matter."

So it was that Thorsvenn pulled the sledge and Signe down the mountain to Eidfjord and Utne.

A Winter Celebration

Signe now visited each of her family in turn. She came first to her mother's house, for Eidfjord is the nearest the mountains. Signe stayed there two days and a night. Ragnhild was an old woman at this time, with failing eyes and white hair. She no longer walked easily. She greeted her daughter well nonetheless and said, "Few will think it wise that you stay in Norway. Still, some of us are like that."

"Yes," said Signe. "I fear that's true."

The time came to leave. Signe asked Ragnhild if she might have some of the piano wire Olav had once brought to Eidfjord. Ragnhild agreed and said, "This is a small thing you ask, when I'd rather give a great one."

"It seems small; still, I have large hopes for it."

Signe left. Ragnhild later spoke these lines:

> Signe's not   safe with life
> Grayly eyed   Odin's child
> Godly men   greet me well
> Wish my daughter   dead.

Signe traveled on to Na and to see her daughter Ashild. She stopped there a night and a day. After a time, Signe said to Ashild, "I remember that Edvard once gave you a pair of binoculars. I wonder if I might have them for a time."

"They're yours, naturally, if you want," said Ashild. "I could wish you did not ask them of me, though, when you mean to use them in some dangerous way. No daughter likes to help her mother to death."

"That's a thing few mothers need help with," said Signe.

· · ·

Signe next went across the fjord to Michael's house at Ullensvang. She stayed there two days and three nights. She and
Michael spoke of many things, of America and past times, and
as well of Michael's sailing ships.

When the two were ready to part, Michael asked, "Is there
any word I can carry to my father from you, in case I should see
him again?"

Signe said at first that there was not. Then she smiled and
said, "Tell him this, that his churchmen can't be worse than
mine."

Michael said, "I have also a small present for you. It's this
snake I caught in the summer, and have kept for you ever
since."

Signe took the snake and said, "It won't surprise me if this is
the best thing I have for the spring." She made up a bag for the
snake so that it could ride next to Thorsvenn and so keep warm.
She also milked it of venom. Then Signe went on to her house
with Olav in Utne.

A little before Signe arrived home, word came to Einar's house
that she was abroad in the fjordlands. Helgi and Bjorn went to
their father. Helgi said, "Now we have the chance to settle our
grievance with cousin Signe for all time. I say we should go over
this very day and do it."

"No," replied Einar, "that you cannot. She's no outlaw till the
spring. Even then, you'll need a rightful jury to take the law to
her; or else, you'll be in the wrong yourselves. At any rate, you'll
find she's no second-rate enemy."

Bjorn said, "You sound like an old and broken man, Father.
We can wait for the spring well enough. But I think it's only
right if we go over and tweak the tiger's tail for her. Then she'll
know she doesn't stand to get free from us easily."

Helgi agreed with his brother. They crossed the fjord together
and came to Olav's house soon after Signe arrived, and just as
Olav himself came home for the day. Einar's sons knew that they

must not harm anyone then and there; they came only as far as the door. Signe met them with a cooking knife in one hand, and said, "It seems you're quick to hear every rumor, even with your mother dead."

Helgi replied, "We've come to tell you what all decent people think, that you're a woodlouse of a woman to be here still."

And Bjorn said, "It's your good luck that we care more for the gods than you do. Otherwise, you'd never get safely back to your mountain."

Signe started to reply to her cousins. But Olav stepped between her and Einar's sons. He said, "You've brought insult to my doorstep; but we won't be goaded into a fight, even so, since that's what you seem to hope for. But it's a good guess that things will turn out worse for you than for Signe in the end."

Helgi said, "What's bound to happen will, but not with the help of a sagging branch like you." Helgi and Bjorn left soon after. They seemed well pleased with their words.

Signe and Olav spoke into the night. Signe said she meant to go back alone to live with Inger until the judgment of the spring.

"There's much to regret in your words," said Olav. "I'd much sooner to leave Hardanger with you and go on with our life together somewhere else; or, if that cannot be, to stand together against what's to come."

"I've never seen you strike a blow in anger," said Signe, "and I think it will be your death if you do now. It's not right that you die for my brother, either. There's something I'd rather you did for me, in any case—that's to carry the case against my enemies to the Thing after I'm dead. Between us, we may bring most of them to grief."

Olav was still uncertain. "Will they not have it right, those who say it's unmanly for me to leave you alone in this?"

"Would you prefer to forget a lifetime of peace?" asked Signe. "It's much the better thing to act now as you have throughout. It's the way of my life to be outside the laws one way or another, and only right that I test my cunning against the strength of my cousin and his friends. But you, Olav, you must use the gifts fated to you, not the ones that have fallen to me."

Olav saw that Signe would not change her mind. He said, "You won't let me to stand with you in the spring, and I'll not stand against you now."

But Signe was not yet finished. She said, "There is another thing. I mean to take a toll of the first people to pass the way to Inger's in the spring. You know that children sometimes plan things their own way, and that ours may be as headstrong as any. I beg you to be sure that none of them follows me up the mountain."

"I'll do as you ask in that, too," said Olav. "All will be well if my voice is as strong as I think it." A little later he said, "You must grant me one thing if you must be alone in this—that you will take my throwing knife with you. Then you may not forget me when the worst comes."

Signe laughed and said, "How should I forget you? But this knife of yours will be the last thing I keep to myself."

In the days that followed, Signe asked Ann to make some wooden planking. "It needn't bear much more weight than itself," said Signe.

Ann made the planks, and also gave Signe a bow she had made herself. "There's more skill in the bow," said she.

It was not long then until Yule. Signe and Olav held a feast for their children as they were used to do each year. This time the feast was grander than usual. Each person brought some special thing to it.

All passed well until everyone had finished eating. Then Signe stood and said, "I hope that you have enjoyed this time of ours together. In the morning I shall leave you to recome the mountains for the winter; no one can know whether or in what state I may return. So now is the time for me to bid you farewell. Then I can leave without sadness.

"For the rest of the winter, I would have you treat me as no longer living and not yet dead. I will that none of you raise a hand to defend me as you would during my lifetime; and also that you do nothing to venge me as if I were dead. I face now my own fate which grew as far away as Africa and as long ago as most of you cannot recall. You'll do both yourselves and me a disservice to take a part of what is mine alone. In any case, you must remember that you have already played a fit part in my fate because of the lives we've had together and because of the many gifts I have from you.

"But let us talk more pleasantly. I have gifts also, and for each of you to remember me by—or to use however you like." She gave out her presents, ones she had long been saving to herself. Each person there said that a living person had never given so much of herself away. There were toasts then until late in the night.

Early in the morning, well before first light, Signe rose from her bed with Olav and went out to be sure her sledge was well balanced and Michael's snake well packed. She harnessed Thorsvenn and recame the house to take her leave of Olav Whitebrow the Southlander.

Winter Preparations

Signe stopped once only on her way back to Ingers-stead. This was at the house of Jussi the Finn, who lived then at Ovreeidfjord. He lived just at the beginning of the road up to Inger's, in a house with a stone wall around the yard. Signe called on him and said, "We've always been friends."

"That's true," said Jussi the Finn.

"I have a thing to ask of you, that you let no one to take this road from the time of the thaw until a jury comes after me." She described a little of what she planned to do.

Jussi said, "I will do this for you."

∙   ∙   ∙

Signe went on to Inger's place in the snow.

Life at Inger's house went on much as before. Aunt and niece talked off and then during the evenings; Signe painted during the short day, and sometimes at night, by the light of some kerosene lamps she had from home. One of the paintings was of herself inside the hut. She painted it so that it would fit exactly into one of the windows. Otherwise, she painted from her memories of many places, usually in panels of three parts, and, as well, two pictures of Inger.

All the winter Signe kept her snake in its box and in the right places for it to wake well in the spring. The last thing she did was to practice throwing the knife she had from Olav.

People in the fjordland below also thought on the spring. Einar's sons, Helgi and Bjorn, urged their father to take the lead in making up a jury to face Signe. They reminded him of the many troubles Signe had brought to them, and also of Gunilla's feeling when she had been alive. But Einar held back; he said he was coming an old man, and also that he did not trust Signe to be a fair enemy.

At last, Knut Magnis-priest came to see Einar. Einar mentioned Signe. Knut was quick to reply: "That woman defies gods and men as well. I don't know why so few speak of bringing her down, even now."

"Signe's no friend to me," said Einar. "But I can't see she does much harm in the mountains."

Knut said, "It's kind for you to think that. But the truth is that she's fated to make harm all her life, and for you most of all. You'll never rest at peace while she lives."

Einar looked at Knut and at his sons. At last he said, "I can't stand against all of you. Still, Magni had better stand my side and the jury's, or we'll have much to regret."

• • •

Einar went first to his brother Ulf. He said, "Our cousin Signe doesn't mean to leave Norway. It's up to us to find a jury and take the law to her."

"It's Olav's wife you speak of," said Ulf, "and my friend and cousin. There's nothing to say we have to carry a bad law further than it deserves."

"It's the law, nonetheless," said Einar. "In any case, this matter between Signe and me has been a thing of blood for years; you should stand by your brother in it."

"Not when Signe is also my close kinswoman, and you mean to fight to the death."

"Your son once had me to thank for his life. Perhaps you grudge me that now."

"This claim you do have on me," said Ulf. "I've no choice but to follow where you lead. Still, it's unwise that you ask this of me; I'll ask no one to help in it. If you find the rest of a jury, I'll join you."

"It seems to me," said Einar, "that you're something of a miser about this."

Einar spent three weeks finding young men with daring enough to stand against Signe. Many refused, some from fear, and some because they thought the right lay with Signe. But others thought Signe a dangerous woman and felt it a duty to join against her. Among these were Rolf Kjells-son; Aksel Johans-son; and the blood friends, Per of Jondal and Gunnar the Tall. Goran the Swede had his own reasons to mislike Signe. Karsten Eigils-son said he would come for money, as did Eyvind Gaptooth. This Eyvind was the cleverest of the men to go with Einar, an ugly man of several scars; few enemies escaped him unscathed.

Stein Lars-son and Jan the Southlander both owed money to Einar. He promised to forgive them their debts if they joined him. Thorkel Lace-ear went also; he thought to please Knut Magnis-priest.

Einar told these men to join him at Kvanndal on the first day of Signe's outlawry. He sent word to Ulf that a jury would stand ready then.

Ulf now came to Olav and told him how matters stood. Olav said, "You must look for me to stand by my fate as you do by yours. It's likely we'll be enemies from now on."

"It was mine to tell you, in any case."

Olav turned away and would listen no further.

Spring

Now the snow melts and all the world quickens, not least Signe's plans. Just after the snow melts, she goes down to the bridge. She takes off the old planks, loosened from the fall, and replaces them with the light ones Ann has made new. She takes the old planks behind a stone wall nearby, until they cannot be seen from the road. She puts bits of mud and dry leaves over the new planks so there is nothing odd to mark the spot. She also takes some stakes, sharpens the ends, puts them in poison; she set the stakes into the river bed beneath the bridge and anchors them with rocks against the current.

Now she goes up to the tunnel she noted before. She takes Ragnhild's piano wire and threads it across the road, at the height of the neck of a man on horseback. She tacks the wire to the walls of the tunnel, and also to the loosened roof above.

After this Signe returns to Ingers-stead. In the barn she sets up the bow so that an arrow can be loosed by pulling a string that runs across the yard. She tests the device to know how it works and where it is aimed. She puts marks on the ground to show the path of an arrow and covers the string over with loose dirt. In the shed, she digs a small hole and puts all her paintings from the winter into it, save only the one of herself. She retouches this last painting in the afternoon light.

Now, she tells Inger, all is ready.

• • •

On the first day that Signe was an outlaw, Einar's jury gathered at Kvanndal. Einar fed them well, and the next day they came as far as Eidfjord and Ulf's farm. Here they stayed overnight.

On the morning following, Ulf went to the house of Jussi the Finn and said, "I know you are the man who lives nearest this road to the mountains. What can you tell me of it if we want to go up to Ingers-stead?"

Jussi replied, "No man has passed it so far this year. But it's most often been clear by now in past years. If you think to take ten or twelve men with you, it should be safe enough."

Ulf thanked Jussi for his help and said he meant to take enough people to help along the way. Jussi said nothing to that, but turned away to work in his own field.

Ulf and Einar spent the rest of that day gathering together food and weapons enough to be sure not to run short on the way.

The jury set off early the next day. They reached Signe's bridge in the middle of the morning, with Rolf Kjells-son in the lead. Rolf got well out onto the bridge before he fell through. His horse broke a leg, and Rolf himself fell onto two of Signe's stakes. He stayed under the bridge only a moment, however; then the current carried him some way downstream before it brought him to shore. The others in the jury stopped to care for Rolf and to take counsel.

Two of the men wanted to call the trip off. They thought it clear that Signe's cleverness was of a dangerous sort. But Einar said, "We can't let the first sight of blood drive us off. It was a lot of work for Signe to rebuild this bridge, and it hasn't killed even one of us."

They agreed that Jan the Southlander should stay behind to find a way to bring Rolf to a doctor.

The rest of the party rode on. They now passed through a

woods. Ulf told them to go at a walk and to watch the ground carefully for further traps; the ground seemed him good for ambush. The others did as he said, and avoided more difficulty until they came out of the woods and started up the fell. Ulf now thought it safe to trot once more.

Stein Lars-son was in the lead when they came to the tunnel. He went half the way through before his horse reared and whimpered. Just after that, there came a tumble of rock from the roof of the tunnel, enough almost to block the way. It was hard for the others to see what had happened; the tunnel was dark. Most of them thought some great witchcraft must be at work. Even Ulf said, "It's hard business when stones bury a stone." But when they dug out Stein's body, they found his head almost parted from his body; and then they found the whole of Signe's machine.

Eyvind Gaptooth now spoke: "She's clever, this one. It seems to me we've already paid a sore price for an errand we should never have begun."

Einar came into a rage at these words. He replied, "This Magni-cursed cousin of mine has hurt one man and killed another, aside from all her other crimes. We can't turn back without getting something in blood from her, when we've already paid such a price."

The nine who were left in the jury cleared the path of Signe's stonework and told Goran the Swede to stay behind to bury their dead comrade. The rest took to their horses once more; but Eyvind and Thorkel Lace-ear would go no further unless Ulf and Einar rode in front. Eyvind said, "If there are any more of these surprises, it's best to have the wisest among us to meet them first."

The Battle

In the days of outlawry, Signe took to using her binoculars to watch the upcoming path from a rock that overlooked it. When the jury came out of the tunnel, she saw them, and marked that they were only eight strong. But she knew they would soon be come, and probably not in the best of humors. She went to Inger and said, "They've lost little time in coming after me, these suitors, sleek and fat as they are. It's a pleasure to have such eager guests. But you must leave now or not at all. You can't help me here, and there are two things I would have you take to people in Hardanger."

Signe went inside and brought out a letter and the snake box they had cared for during the winter. She said, "This letter is for Olav to tell him where to find the things I've left for him. This other is for Einar, a welcome-home token, as it were. Tell his housepeople that you've brought it from Knut Magnis-priest, and that they must keep it near the fire and let no one but Einar open it."

Inger took her trusted Thorsvenn and left her own *saeter* behind. She went down to Hardanger by a back way, one of those she had shown Signe years before.

Signe stands and watches her aunt, then goes back to the house. She puts her own portrait in the window, checks that the bow in the barn is ready, and makes her way to the shed with her paints and her knife.

It is now four in the afternoon. Einar and Ulf lead their party up to Inger's farm. They tie their horses some way down the path, then creep closer. They can see Signe quite clearly in the window of the house.

Ulf says, "I think Gunnar and I should go ahead of the rest and try to surprise her."

Einar says, "That's a good thought; she can hardly complain if we take her unaware, after the way she's treated with us."

Ulf now goes up on the left and Gunnar on the right. When they reach the window, each man slashes at it with a sword. But their steel finds only glass and canvas. Gunnar says, "The woman's cheated us again."

The others stand now and cross the open ground to see what

has gone wrong. They are half the way across when they hear the sound of an arrow hitting flesh. Aksel falls. He says, "Einar, this is your doing that I have my death. But I don't think I'll wait long before you join me."

The others cannot at once tell where the arrow has come from, but mill around the yard in all directions. Ulf calls, "The barn; break the door." All the jury rushes at once; they find no one inside, but only the bow. Eyvind and Ulf try to make the others quiet for a moment, but they are hardly heard.

Karsten yells that everything must be burned. He, Gunnar, and Per strike sparks and set some of the hay alight. Everyone must come out of the barn after that. But the three who put it to fire bring out torches to use on the other buildings as well. They go over to the house first and light the roof.

While the jurymen busy themselves in this way, Signe steps out of the shed. Einar and his men turn. Signe throws her knife and catches Gunnar the Tall between the ribs. No one understands what has happened for a moment. Gunnar has not the time to say anything. He looks at Signe, takes two steps toward her, and looks at his shirt. He sees the blood spreading over it and, with a look of surprise, dies.

Einar speaks to Signe: "We have you now."

"So it seems," says Signe, "but you haven't much of your jury left."

The men fell on Signe then and hacked her to death. They burned the shed to the ground and slaughtered all the animals. They started to bury their dead. It was then that they found a note stuck to Gunnar's new knife. It said:

> Fourfold the price   you pay, landsmen
> To say sentence   and solve my fate.
> Was it worthy   my wiles to match
> With stupid strength   stymied on the path?

The jurymen buried their comrades; but Signe's body they took up and put on a high stone, so that birds might pick her bones clean. Per said, "We may as well leave white bones for the white-brow."

That is all that is told of the fight at Ingers-stead.

Homecoming

The jury camped the night somewhat down the mountain from Inger's. In the morning they recame the fjordlands. Some of the men went to their homes. But Ulf went first to Ragnhild. He said, "Your daughter is dead, though I could have wished it otherwise. Still, she killed three men before she fell."

Ragnhild replied, "Then you've bought her life cheaply."

Einar and Eyvind stopped at the inn in Kinsarvik to eat a meal before coming home. They told the whole story of their work on the mountain. Then Eyvind said, "The odd thing is that we cheated old Signe at the last. She boasted of killing four of us, and only three have died, though it's true enough a fourth lies hurt."

Ivar still kept the inn. He said, "I've heard that Signe sometimes found it difficult to count when it came to important things. But I've always been told that she was more apt to be generous than stingy at such times."

The others in the inn laughed at that. But Einar seemed ill at ease. He left to take his boat home soon after.

When Einar reached Kvanndal, his sons greeted him. Helgi said, "Your victory's bound to be a famous one, Father. Already someone's brought a package from Knut Magnis-priest for it."

Einar said, "There's no good to glory in someone's death,

even of such a one as Signe. Beside, three of my fellows lie dead as well."

Bjorn said, "'Dearly bought, dear to the heart.'"

Einar was tired by now and thought no more of it when his sons pressed him to open his package. He unwrapped it, opened the top, and put his hand under the paper to bring out what might be inside. But the package bit him full in the hand; he pulled away and saw the serpent coiled there. He said, "This isn't the sort of welcome I hoped for; I fear I'll soon be as cold as now my hand is hot."

The sons killed the snake and found some writing in the box. This said, "From the grave I greet you, Cousin. As ever, Signe."

They called for a doctor. But he had no cure when he came, and Einar grew weak. He called his sons to him and also the serving man who had taken the package. That man was called Svein. Einar asked Svein to describe the person who had brought the package, which he did.

Einar said, "This can only be Inger. She wasn't found on the mountain."

Soon Einar slept; he did not wake again.

In the morning, Helgi and Bjorn went to Kinsarvik to look for Inger. They thought her too old to have gone far. They found she was at the inn, and had been all the night before. They were unhappy with Ivar that he had known this and said nothing to Einar about it. But they went first to Inger's room and struck her down. They came back to take care of Ivar. But the innkeeper had three heavy men by his side; Einar's sons made no more threats after that and went home to Kvanndal.

This same day, Rolf Kjells-son died. His wounds were not the sort that usually kill. It happened, however, that the nurse who changed his bandages was a student of Signe's; most nurses in Hardanger in those days had studied with Signe, or else with her mother. Some say that this nurse was more devoted to her teacher than to her patient. But when Rolf's wounds grew worse and killed him, none could show foul play.

Ann and Olav

News of Signe's death came to Utne even before Inger died. Olav heard it in silence; he had expected nothing else. Later, he said no more when he was told of Inger's death. Ann then asked him, "Have you lost all your hopes, Father, that you say nothing to murder?"

"What should I say," asked Olav, "when it's words against knives."

"That I don't know. But it cannot be right that you despair, you who sat up a whole summer to save my eyes."

"I promised Signe to fight her enemies at the Thing, and so I will. I can't see much good it will do, either."

On the second night following, Ann rose and took Signe's old boat out onto the fjord. It was then nearly a full moon, and all the lands could be seen clearly. Ann sailed to Kvanndal and beached the boat some way to the west of Einar's old farm.

Ann walked up to Einars-stead, where now only Helgi and Bjorn lived. There was no sign of the Einars-sons. Ann set fire to their barn in several places. It was a dry year, and even the sod roof smoldered. Ann stayed long enough to be sure that the building could not be saved, then came away to her boat.

Helgi and Bjorn had been drinking with a neighbor. They saw the light from their own farm, red against the white moonlight, and came running back to it. They could see that the fire was hopeless, so they took bows from the house and arrows. Helgi set off down the road to the east; Bjorn went along the fjord to find the places where boats might have landed.

Bjorn it was who found Ann. She had just set out onto the fjord and was still trimming the sail. Bjorn shot three arrows at her. One struck her in the back and another in the leg. The second was the more serious wound. Ann was soon weak from shock and loss of blood. She still made her way back to Utne and up the hill to Olav's house. Bjorn had to be content to let her go; his boats lay some way off, and he was not a very good sailor.

Olav woke to find his daughter at the door, almost faint, with an arrow still in her leg. He brought her to bed, dressed the wound in her back, and at last removed the arrow in her leg with a sterile knife. Ann was asleep through most of the time.

At first light and before the late-night mist had yet lifted from the water, Olav went to several of his neighbors. They agreed to stand with him in case anyone should cross the fjord after Ann. One of them said he would watch for boats; another went off to Eidfjord to tell Ulf Pers-son what had fallen and to ask him to visit Olav. That man also sent the doctor to Olav's house.

Olav recame home. He found Ann asleep and looking pale.

The doctor came with the afternoon. He dressed the wounds a second time and gave Olav medicine to give Ann.

Ann woke in the evening. After a time, she said, "I've done something of what was needed, Father."

Olav looked at his daughter and then said, "What you say now is madness in the midst of madness, when one corpse already lies atop the next. I'd have nothing to live for if you'd been killed at this."

"Then don't let me die, and don't tell me you see no good you can do."

"Very well," said Olav, "I'll fight for your sake as well as for Signe's. But in my own way, and at the Thing, not in some cow field. And you must rest content with that."

"It seems I must rest, in any case," said Ann.

On the day following, Ann had a fever and her breath ran short. Olav feared for her life; but the doctor said she was a healthy child and could live through so small a trouble.

Ulf arrived on this day. He stayed only a short time. He and Olav agreed to speak with their relatives and friends, and to allow no more killing or looting before the Thing met. Any offense in the meantime was to be atoned at triple the usual price.

All through the spring, Ann stayed weak and sick in her bed. Her leg went red, and in the end was always somewhat lame. Olav's eyebrows now went as white as his hair; he spent all his days at home, or walking nearby, thinking of the Thing to come.

But there were no further deaths during this time.

Trials at the Thing

The time for the Thing now comes and with it people from all Hardanger to Kinsarvik. It is said that this was the largest Thing in Hardanger up to that time.

The first day for hearing criminal suits came. The Lawspeaker was then Hakon of Odda. Several people rose to speak, but Olav Whitebrow claimed the right to be first; he had once before been Lawspeaker of the Thing. This seemed important at the time; the first speaker is able to lay charge against only one person, but it was thought that Olav would charge his old friend Ulf and convict him, and so keep him from speaking later. The rest of Einar's jury were not held in high regard as lawyers.

But Olav spoke in this way: "I would not have it said that I gave charge against a man who had not the chance to be heard. Therefore, I shall take the smallest matter first and save the major ones for later.

"Whatever else has happened this year, we can agree that Einar's Law has shown itself false. I say nothing for the moment about the rights of the cases we shall hear. In all cases, our trouble has grown from the time that Einar's Law was used to kill Edvard Ragnhilds-son. Since then many more have died—

my wife Signe, her aunt Inger, all those who died at Signe's hands in the mountains, Einar himself. I know little of the gods; but a law that makes so many peaceful people kill, and so many living ones dead, is a bad law.

"Let us agree that Einar's Law is no law, as a third of us thought when first it was raised. After that, the trials can fall as they will; at least we'll have done some good."

Most of the Thing thought Olav had thrown away his chance of speaking first. It was the custom by then to let bad laws die of neglect; even most of the priests disliked Einar's Law now, and it was little likely it would ever be used again. It seemed that Olav must be so downcast from the events of the spring that he no longer hoped to win the other cases. Some said he had never been the same after his daughter was hurt. And Eyvind said to Ulf, "This seems a good beginning for us."

But Ulf replied, "Perhaps. But you've never lived in the same house with that man."

Only Knut Magnis-priest stood to defend Einar's Law. He said, "It's true enough that people have died for Einar's Law. But it is the people who have killed each other; the law has hurt no one except by right. Edvard and Signe defied both the law and the gods, and got no more than they deserved. The men who carried the law to Signe acted rightly; we must be glad that so many were willing to stand against her, even when they knew how hard-souled she was.

"This law is part of what we know of the will of the gods; it's not something to be turned aside lightly, especially not now when it's helped us against two of those who cared nothing for our laws or for our land. Let us not lose it just when it shows its worth."

The law now came to a vote. There were two people voting with Olav and against the law for every one who stood by Knut.

The Thingholder for the year was a man called Eigil Vanskel-ligheten. He said, "Einar's Law is tried and found to be no law."

Lawspeaker Hakon now called on Ulf Pers-son to speak.

Ulf said, "I lay charge against Olav Whitebrow and also against his family members, Ann and Ashild Olavs-datters, Michael Signes-son, and Ragnhild Arnes-datter, that they gave aid and comfort to the outlaw Signe Ragnhilds-datter; also that they gave her the weapons she used to kill members of the jury charged to bring the law to her; and finally that they stand to account for those murders themselves, since they meant for Signe to use the weapons as she did."

Hakon began to name the judge of forty to hear the case. But Olav rose and said, "I think we have no case to answer."

Olav argued that Signe had been wrongly called an outlaw because Einar's Law was not a true law; further, that even if she had been an outlaw, she had the right to defend herself, "like any other Norseman"; that, therefore, there were no murders to be accounted.

Ulf now saw why Olav had charged Einar's Law first of all. He was not yet willing to give in, however, and said, "You overreach yourself, friend Olav; Signe never broke Einar's Law, but only the one against sacrilege, which is quite separate."

Olav stood again and said that Signe had been wrongly convicted of sacrilege. Her offense was to bury her brother who was said to be an outlaw. But Edvard in turn had broken no law, but only the false act of Einar's. There could be no guilt in burying him.

"Rightly or not," said Ulf, "Signe faced trial and was found to have guilt. That made her an outlaw regardless."

"No," said Olav. "The judge acted in the belief that a false law was true. Their judgment is void, as if the trial had never been."

Hakon ruled for Olav in this. Ulf then called on the former Lawspeakers to overturn Hakon's judgment. Olav did not sit with his fellows; they ruled with Hakon even so.

Thingholder Eigil now said, "Olav Whitebrow and his family have no case to answer."

Hakon next called on Olav once more. Olav rose and laid charge against Ulf Pers-son and his six fellows of the jury for the murder of Signe Ragnhilds-datter and the burning of Inger's house. Witness to these charges was brought.

The seven jurors chose Ulf to speak for them. Ulf did not deny that they had killed Signe and burned the farm. Instead, he spoke in this way: "I ask you to think more deeply on this matter. We had no thought of murder when we went up the mountain, we seven. We thought Signe an outlaw; we wanted only to carry the law to her as we thought we had the right and the duty to do. Who among you thought we had not that right? If we were in the wrong, we had most of you in company with us. But, in fact, we and you were in the right as far as anyone knew it. More should not be asked of us.

"We burned the farm, that is so. But we had already seen three of our number fall to the most cunning of traps, and sought to save ourselves from more.

"Perhaps we are guilty if the law is strict. But if so, it is not the usual sort of guilt, but rather the misfortune into which anyone of you could have fallen. You will do best not to think of our deeds alone, but of what we meant as well. Then you can well find us without guilt; or, if that is not possible, you can show mercy in the sentence.

"Only seven of our jury have been charged; five of us lie dead on this venture already. Each of us has lost a close friend at the least; I have lost my brother. Even if we were wrong, we have paid a dear price already."

Olav stood to reply. He said, "The words of Ulf Pers-son are those of a wise and gentle man. But the words themselves are not wise. He says we were all wrong in thinking Signe an outlaw. Perhaps it is so. But not all of us thought to kill her. For the rest of us, it matters nothing how well we judged the matter. But the burden is greater for this jury of Ulf's, who chose to lift the sword. They cannot call back their deeds; they have not the luxury to be wrong.

"Ulf asks mercy, mercy for good intent. But he and his men are not children caught at some small mistake. They are men who chose to kill, and who set loose other killings. A good woman—the finest of women—lies dead at their hands, and unburied, but she will not go unatoned.

"If you treat these men as the killers they are, and make them pay the price anyone would for the crime, others will think before they act in the future. They will say to themselves, 'How will it seem if we are wrong?' They will learn to honor the law and not merely to serve her. But let these men go, and there must still be vengeance for Signe; and the new law of Hardanger will be: Stand for your own, fight for your own, for no one will stand by you, even in a fair cause."

The case now went to the judge. In the end all the seven were judged to have guilt. The sentence was the same in each case, that the man be outlawed for three years and made to give up half his property to pay for the blood guilt.

That was the last case heard on that day. In the evening following, Ulf Pers-son came to see Olav at his hut. He said, "Now I see how far friendship counts when people are driven by revenge."

Olav looked at his old friend and said, "We've done no more than we had to, you and I."

Ulf turned away. It seemed to some that he wept.

•   •   •

The next morning Olav claimed the right to continue his suits. He laid charge against Helgi and Bjorn, Einar's sons, that they had killed Inger Arnes-datter. Olav described the crime, and called witness to all that had happened when Helgi and Bjorn came over the fjord to Ivar's inn. There seemed to be no question but that Helgi and Bjorn bore guilt in the matter. But Olav mentioned neither the fire that Ann had set in Einar's old barn, nor any of what had happened to her afterwards. He hoped in this way to keep suit from being laid against Ann in the matter, and was willing to accept a lesser judgment against the Einars-sons.

Helgi and Bjorn spoke in their own defense, one after the other. At last Bjorn said, "We cannot deny what we have done, and would not if we could. We are not so far in the wrong as Olav claims. It was our father who died at Inger's hand; it was Inger's niece who killed our friends on the mountain; it was her family who helped her do it. It is Signe's daughter who thought to kill us while we slept, till we chased her away. Perhaps we did more than was right to kill Inger, though she was certainly a killer herself. But it is not more than one can understand, when we've been hounded early and late by that family, and for many years."

The judge gave it as their judgment that Einar's sons had murdered Inger Arnes-datter as claimed. But they also judged that the two men had acted in the heat of finding their father dead, and so gave them three years as outlaws from Hardanger and ordered them also to give up half their property as payment for blood guilt.

It seemed then that the trials might be over for that year. But Knut Magnis-priest now stood. He laid charge against Ann Olavs-datter that she had burned the barn at Kvanndal and killed many animals. When the time came to give evidence, Bjorn would not speak; he feared that Olav would find a friend to speak against him for the arrows he had shot at Ann. But Helgi spoke openly. Olav saw that there was no defense for his daughter. He said that Ann's deed was at least as justified as those of many others, and that at any rate, hers had killed no one. He also said that she was quite young and ought to be given some allowance on that count.

But the judge thought little of these arguments. They said Ann had guilt by twenty-seven votes to thirteen. Her sentence was two years of outlawry to begin from the time that she was well enough to travel. She was also to pay a fine, large enough to rebuild the barn.

This was the last lawsuit that arose from the death of Edvard Ragnhilds-son and the many things that followed on his death.

After

Olav recame Utne from the Thing. He told Ann the news and said, "I would rather that no case had come against you."

"So I can see," said Ann, "when you left Helgi and Bjorn to go so easily."

"It's true they deserved worse than Ulf," said Olav. "But no weapon is as sharp as one would like, and the law least of all."

Late in the summer, Ann came well enough to leave Hardanger. By that time, Michael Signes-son also wished to travel; he had taken his mother's death badly. The two fared south together and wintered on the coast of France. The next year they sailed on to America. Michael stayed there two winters with his father in Wisconsin before he recame Norway. But Ann stayed on, for six winters in all. She traveled to many places and had, it is said, three adventures. After that, however, she recame Hardanger, she also.

Ulf Pers-son went oversea too, but only as far as Ireland. He left Britt his wife to watch over their children and what was left of their farm at Eidfjord.

Ulf sailed south from Ireland in the summers, as far as the south of Portugal. But most of the year, he stayed at a place called Kilkee and lived from fishing.

The Irish say that Ulf was a lonely man all the time he stayed in their land. They also tell a story of his death in the fall of the last year he was to stay there. Ulf went one day to fish in the ocean from a place that many counted dangerous but that he had often been to before. Three days passed, and then his body was found dead at the place, some way back from the water; he was lying amid some rocks; his skull was broken.

The Irish say that Ulf had taken so many fish from those rocks that the king of all the fish living near that part of Ireland came in person to take Ulf's hook. After a struggle that must have lasted many hours, or perhaps even a whole day, the line parted. Ulf then fell backwards away from the sea and into the rock that killed him. The king of fish also recoiled many kilometers to sea. All the schools that paid him tribute followed him. The Irish say that this story accounts for the fact that fisherman took only a few fish from shore in the next years, but as many as ever from the open sea.

However that is, Olav heard of Ulf's death only in the winter, after he had been made Lawspeaker for the second time. He thereupon gave to Britt all that he had in fines of the farms at Kvanndal and Eidfjord; Ulf's descendants live in those places still.

The rest of the farm at Eidfjord belonged still to Ragnhild Arnes-datter; she had several years more to live. But she preferred to stay with Ashild her granddaughter, or with Olav himself. She was old and frail, almost blind.

Ragnhild made over all her holdings at Eidfjord to Edvard's children. She would give no rights to Shiela the American. Few marked it that Shiela needed her help, in any case.

It happened once while Ragnhild stayed with Olav at Utne that a young man came to seek Olav's advice over some lawsuit or other. The two men talked in the front room for some time before the young man asked Olav who was the old woman he could see in the next room. Olav told him that it was that Ragnhild who had spent so many years in Africa.

The young man said, "So many stories are told of her, I thought she must be dead. It's a pity to see she's outlived her times so far." Then the young man returned to talk of his lawsuit and gave no more thought to Ragnhild. But Olav saw her rise a few minutes later and leave the room.

Olav took the young man into the kitchen and fed him lunch. Then the time came for him to leave. He came to the front door and went out onto the first step. It gave way under his foot; he fell the rest of the way to the ground and caught his foot against a railing on the way, so that he fell with his face in the mud.

Olav said to him, "I fear Ragnhild's never outlived her ears."

Ragnhild died at Utne two years before Ann recame Norway. Olav lived on for many years at the same place, and served as Lawspeaker a third time.

After some years Ann married and brought her husband to live at Olavs-stead.

All the three children of Signe Ragnhilds-datter had children of their own in the end. Some grew to be tall and fair; others grew shorter and brown-haired like Signe herself.

About the Author

CHARLES WHITMORE holds degrees in political science from Haverford College and Yale University. He has taught in the United States and in East Africa. He currently lives with his wife, Christine Nicolai, outside Philadelphia and works as an energy analyst studying the effects of natural gas regulation in the United States. WINTER'S DAUGHTER is his first novel.